SCHOOLED IN MURDER

A Charley Hall Mystery, Book 6

Brenda Gayle

Schooled in Murder
(A Charley Hall Mystery, Book 6)
by Brenda Gayle

Published Internationally by Bowstring Books
Ottawa, Ontario, Canada

LARGE PRINT ISBN 978-1-7387434-4-5

For Alice and all of the Gayle Gazetters.
Your support means more than you know.

"Hurry up, Freddie." Charley Hall pushed open the door to her brother's bedroom. "Hal will be here any mo—"

Freddie Stormont slammed shut the lid of his suitcase but not before Charley caught the glint of light bouncing off something long and shiny. Her shoulders sagged.

"Haven't you heard of knocking?" Freddie scowled through his bristly red beard. "I hear it's all the rage these days."

"Sorry." Charley swallowed her anxiety for her brother's fragile sobriety. "It's just—"

"I know, I know. I'm running behind time. The lecture went long and then the professor wanted to talk to me about including two of my poems in the department's upcoming anthology."

"Oh, Freddie, that's wonderful." Charley

crossed the room and embraced her brother, giving him an extra squeeze to reassure herself that he was home and safe, and everything was going to be all right.

He grinned down at her, and she could see both pride and humour in his blue eyes.

"Do you think you can stand not being the only published writer in the family?" He playfully flicked his finger under her chin. "I know how competitive you are."

She stepped back, purposely avoiding glancing at the suitcase. "I don't think writing for a newspaper even begins to compare to the prestige of literary publication. And I couldn't be happier for you."

"Still, who's the one changing the world with their prose? What are my few stanzas of rhyming couplets compared to the parry and thrust of political and social discourse on the pages of the venerable *Kingston Tribune*?"

Charley's eyes narrowed, but no, he wasn't making fun of her. "I merely report on the cut-and-dried actions of what people do every day. You look for meaning. You give hope. You explore the very essence of what it means to be human. Tomorrow my words will end up in the dust bin, replaced by other stories, which will again be forgotten by the time the next edition rolls off the presses. But your poetry will live on to be read and re-read for... who knows, maybe centuries."

"Unless it's skewered by some snooty literary critic." He'd said it flippantly, but she heard the apprehension behind his words.

Yes, there was always danger in publishing. She'd experienced backlash from people who were unhappy about what she'd written. That was to be expected in the newspaper business. For Freddie, his poems were so personal that an attack on them would feel like an attack on his very being.

"I read in the newspaper that there's to be a total lunar eclipse tonight," she said to change the subject. "With the full moon, it should be quite something to see."

"A full moon *and* a total eclipse? I hadn't heard that." Freddie frowned.

"Why the look? It's only the earth's shadow passing across the surface of the moon."

"Is it though?" Freddie cocked a brow and lowered his voice. "There's something primal about a full moon, and for millennia the blood-stained face from an eclipse has evoked mystery and a fear of impending doom."

Charley shivered at her brother's ominous tone. Then with a wink and a grin, he broke the mood. She swatted at him, annoyed to be taken in by such silliness. "Can we go now?"

Freddie picked up his suitcase and motioned for her to precede him, reciting from the Old Testament's *Book of Joel* as they descended to the main floor. "And I will shew wonders in the heavens and in the earth, blood, and fire, and pillars of smoke / The sun shall be turned into darkness, and the moon into blood, before the great and terrible day of the Lord come."

Even though she knew he was teasing, the hairs rose on the back of Charley's neck and a strange sense of foreboding fell over her. Was it any wonder her brother had rejected the family business of journalism, choosing instead to pursue a more creative outlet for his storytelling?

Freddie had always been the more sensitive of the two of them. It was a miracle that he'd survived three years in a German POW camp and then a months-long death march across Poland and Czechoslovakia before being freed by the Allies.

"Looks like Hal's already here," Freddie said, nodding at the grey woollen overcoat slung atop the newel post at the bottom of the staircase. He placed his large, tan-coloured leather suitcase beside the smaller, soft-sided blue tartan bag she'd brought down earlier.

She stared at his suitcase, her stomach twisting with a familiar dread. She wished she had the x-ray vision of the comic book hero that was so popular these days. But maybe it was better she couldn't see into it. At least this way she could pretend—hope—it wasn't a bottle of whiskey that he'd hidden from her.

"Coming?" Freddie called over his shoulder as he disappeared into the drawing room. “Hal, I’m sorry we kept you waiting. Have you been here long?”

Hal Overstreet rose from the sofa at their entrance. “No apologies needed. I haven’t had the opportunity to visit with your grandmother since my return, so I welcome the delay,” he said smoothly, giving Bessie Stormont a flirtatious wink.

“Hal was just telling me that he’s secured the Liberal party’s nomination to run for Parliament in the next federal election,” Bessie said.

“Maybe it’s the start of a family dynasty,” Charley said. She had mixed feelings about Hal’s political success as it came at the expense of her long-time friend Dan Cannon’s aspirations.

“Perhaps.” Hal shrugged his broad shoulders and motioned for Charley to join him on the sofa. “But my father’s brand of politics is different from my own.”

It was odd, then, that Hal had chosen to shave off his moustache and beard before the nomination process. Now, he looked the spitting image of his father—or how the senator had looked twenty years ago.

“I would certainly hope it’s different,” Freddie said, sinking comfortably into Charley’s favourite *bergère* armchair, “considering he’s been a federal senator for the better part of two decades and has never had to face the electorate.”

“Are you two going to debate politics the whole week?” Charley asked. “Because if so, I’ll need to pack a few more novels in my bag.”

“Perhaps on the drive there.” Hal’s warm grin extended up to his soft brown eyes. “But I promise, once we arrive, you will have my undivided attention.”

“I still think this is all rather unorthodox,” Gran said. “You weren’t invited, Charlotte. You never even had Mr. Bennett as a teacher.”

“The invitation said we could bring a guest,” Hal said.

“And *I* was invited,” Freddie interjected smoothly. “So, I can chaperone my dear sister to ensure her virtue remains intact.”

“It’s not her virtue I’m concerned about,” Bessie said dryly.

“Gran!” Charley said with mock affront.

“You know what I mean.” Bessie raised her chin imperiously to match her tone. “I have full confidence in Hal’s ability to comport himself appropriately; you too, for that matter. I just don’t think it’s proper. And I am quite sure Mr. Bennett’s inclusion of a guest in the invitation was meant for a wife or husband.”

“Then it should have specified as much,” Charley replied petulantly. She didn’t know why she was quibbling with Gran about this. She’d made the very same arguments to Hal when he’d first asked her to join him for the week-long school reunion on Lake Scugog, northeast of Toronto. Although they’d attended the same high school—albeit she four years later—she’d never had Foster Bennett as her English teacher. Always resourceful, Hal had convinced Freddie to implore Charley to change her mind.

It had taken a couple of weeks, but the two of them managed to wear down her resistance. Once she’d agreed to go, however, she found herself looking forward to getting away from Kingston and its slushy mounds of melting snow.

"What a glorious day!" Evelyn Pierrepont, Charley's maternal grandmother, breezed into the room, her cheeks flushed from her daily walk along the shore of Lake Ontario.

Over the past few days, the weather had shown a marked improvement with the temperature more in line with early summer than early spring. It had made it difficult to decide what to pack. The invitation encouraged guests to plan for a lot of outdoor activities, which wasn't all that surprising since Mr. Bennett had also supervised the boys' Outdoor Club. But April was an unpredictable month, and the balmy days could leave as quickly as they arrived. At the last minute, she'd tucked in a thick wool sweater and a pair of extra warm socks.

If the weather held, an early spring might mean the Atlantic sailing routes would open sooner which meant Evelyn would book her passage back to England sooner as well. Charley's chest tightened and she glanced at her brother. Even if he waited until the university's end of term, Freddie's departure wouldn't be too far behind.

"Have you met—" Bessie began.

But Hal had already shot to his feet and was moving toward Evelyn, his hand outstretched, ready to greet her. "Countess Thorton, it's a pleasure. I've heard so much about you."

Charley winced as Evelyn's eyebrows knitted together in obvious disdain at his gaffe. Oh well, what was one more mark against the colonies? How was Hal expected to know the proper manner to address the countess? Of course, if he'd waited until Bessie had finished her introduction, he might have been able to pick up on her clues.

"Lady Evelyn Pierrepont, Countess of Thorton, this is Harold Overstreet, the second, known affectionately as Hal," Bessie interjected. The glee dancing in her eyes belied the mock seriousness of her tone. There was nothing Gran loved more than a breach of aristocratic etiquette, especially if it came at Evelyn's expense.

"You may call me Lady Evelyn. Thorton is the Earldom, not me." Evelyn's nasally accent was clipped, and she pulled her hand back from Hal's almost as soon as their fingers touched. Clearly, she didn't think Hal was a good match for her granddaughter.

Gran didn't think so either. But it wasn't because she disliked Hal—Bessie liked him a great deal. No, her disapproval stemmed from her conviction that Charley didn't have the temperament to be a good wife to a politician. Gran had felt the same way about her relationship with Dan Cannon. In the end, Dan had married a woman with the perfect disposition to be a politician's wife.

"I think we should be going," Hal said.

"How long will it take you to get there?" Bessie asked.

"Close to four hours, I'd imagine."

"Rachel has prepared us a picnic basket dinner for the drive," Freddie said.

"Wonderful. It's much appreciated. We're still trying to find a decent cook after we lost our housekeeper. Thank goodness Clarice has some culinary skills." Hal turned to

Evelyn and added, "Clarice is my father's new wife."

"It is a struggle to find reliable help, especially since the end of the war," Bessie said.

"I'd have thought that would make it easier," Charley muttered, but apparently not as quietly as she'd thought. Everyone was staring at her. "Well, with all the women being displaced from their jobs by the returning soldiers, wouldn't you think there'd be a glut of them needing to resume working as domestics?"

"I thought you liked your new job editing the women's pages," Freddie said.

"I do, but it wasn't my choice to leave the city beat, now, was it?"

"I think it's admirable that women these days want to get out and learn something about the world before marrying and having children," Hal said. "I'd hate to think of the predicament Father and I would be in without Clarice."

Charley bit the inside of her cheek to stop herself from responding. The only reason

Clarice was able to cook for Hal and his father was that she hadn't been raised with domestic staff as the rest of them had. Knowing how to shop for groceries and prepare meals had been a matter of survival, not a way station on her road to matrimony.

Hal had lived on his own for several years before returning home a few months ago. Surely, he had those same skills. Shouldn't he have taken on some of the responsibility rather than leaving it all to his stepmother?

Charley would like to think that if she or Freddie were ever in Hal's situation, they'd pitch in and help. She glanced at her brother. Would he, though? The only time she'd seen him anywhere near the kitchen was when he was inquiring about what was on the menu for dinner.

Men!

But was she any better? Aside from making tea and toast, she was completely lost in the kitchen. That wouldn't do anymore. After this trip, she'd talk to Rachel about teaching her how to make a few key dishes—just in case. It would be nice if Freddie and

Hal would do the same, but she was pretty sure any suggestion in that regard would fall on deaf ears. Cooking was women's work.

Charley rose from the sofa. "We should be on our way if we want to make it to the resort before the sun sets." She had four hours to temper her resentment toward the men in her life and adopt a more congenial demeanour for the week. She didn't want to embarrass Hal and Freddie in front of their friends.

But more than anything, Charley wanted to prove Gran wrong.

The sun was starting to dip below the horizon when Hal turned his powder-blue Tucker Torpedo into a long laneway. At least that's what it looked like to Charley. It was hard to differentiate this winding gravel road from the winding gravel road they'd been on for the past half-hour—ever since they'd left Highway 7 somewhere around Port Perry.

"Yes, this is it. I'm sure of it," Freddie said, tapping the map on his lap.

Charley leaned forward and craned her neck to look out the front window but all she could see were trees, trees, and more trees.

She was in a much better mood, thanks in no small part to the delicious chicken sandwiches and lemon pound cake Rachel had sent with them. She'd allowed the baritone voices in the front seat to drift over her but hadn't taken part in the conversation except to answer specific questions directed at her. She was looking forward to this week away more than she'd wanted to admit to herself. It was the first vacation she'd taken in six years that she could truly enjoy, no longer consumed by the nagging fear for the well-being of her brother or his best friend, Theo, the man she'd married. It had been difficult enough when they'd enlisted and went to England, but the devastating news that they were missing after the Dieppe landing in 1942 had haunted every aspect of her life. It had taken Freddie over a year to return home after the end of the war, and another two years before he could tell her that Theo had died on that beach in '42.

Her brother had come so far.

But if he'd brought a bottle?

No, she wasn't going to go looking for trouble. She'd keep a watchful eye on him this week. She'd make certain he was all right.

"There!" Freddie pointed to a large, two-storey structure emerging from the shadow of twilight.

"Is Dan here?" Charley asked as Hal eased to a stop beside a familiar Woody station wagon.

"Maybe." Freddie angled his body to see her in the back seat. "Have you spoken with him recently?"

She shook her head. The last time she'd seen him had been the dinner party he and Meredith had hosted for Hal's sister, Poppy. She hadn't been avoiding him exactly, but she hadn't known how to break it to him that Hal was going after the same political nomination he was. "I didn't think he ever had Mr. Bennett as a teacher. No, I'm sure he didn't. Mr. Bennett only taught grades 12 and 13 and we were both in Mr. Littlestone's class those years."

Hal opened the passenger door and extended his hand to help her out. "I imagine there will be quite a few Kingston Collegiate graduates here. Mr. Bennett was a very popular teacher."

"And he'd been there for decades, hadn't he?" Freddie hoisted his suitcase out of the trunk. "He only retired this past Christmas, I heard."

"I read in the newspaper that his parents left this resort to him and his brother in their will," Hal said, ignoring Charley's protest and keeping hold of her suitcase as well as his own. "That could be the reason he finally decided to, although I can't imagine why, at his age, he'd want to take on something like this."

"I agree. He's got to be into his sixties by now, wouldn't you think?" Freddie asked. "He seemed ancient when we had him, and that was what—fifteen years ago? Longer for you, Hal."

Charley noted only four other cars and an old pick-up truck in the parking lot. Perhaps the rest of the former students were coming tomorrow or Friday. She turned her attention to the resort building—a long, two-storey wood and stone structure with a green tin roof. There were noticeable gaps along the top rail of the carved wooden balcony that ran the building's length, and the green painted trim around the windows and doors looked like it could use a touch-up. Faded black paint on a large wooden sign whispered rather than announced Bennett's Family Resort. The sign swung awkwardly from its post as it was missing several links of chain needed to hang level.

Rustic. She imagined that would be how the *Trib*'s travel writer would describe the place if he was being generous.

"Welcome," a woman wearing a brown winter coat and red toque called from behind a long counter out as they entered.

Charley hung back as Hal and Freddie approached her.

The interior reception area was dimly lit. More atmosphere? She shivered at the breeze sneaking in through the rough-hewn wood plank walls and pulled her coat tighter around her body. The well-worn stone floor didn't help. She could feel the cold radiating up through the soles of her black leather oxfords. What had happened to the warm weather of Kingston? They hadn't travelled that far north.

"How many rooms will you be needing?"

the woman—Bonnie, according to the pin on her collar—asked after Hal had rhymed off the names in their party.

"Three," Hal said.

Bonnie frowned as she turned and took down three keys hanging on the wall behind her. Her eyebrows knitted together as she concentrated on recording the room numbers beside their names. "We're putting everyone on the second floor."

"How many are you expecting this week?" Charley asked as she accepted her key.

"I don't remember the exact number of people, but we were fixing to set up nine guest rooms. I do know that much."

"Don't you have a list of the guests?" Hal asked.

"Mr. Foster... That's how we've always referred to the boys—Mr. Foster and Mr. Fraser—to differentiate them from their father, who was Mr. Bennett." She paused and took a breath. "Anyway, Mr. Foster sent me the guest list in the post, and I was sure I'd brought it with me, but I can't seem to find it." Pink tinged her cheeks as her gaze travelled the length of the pristine countertop before returning to Hal. "If it was to be nine rooms, then there's one more party expected after you lot."

"Really?" Hal frowned. "I'd have thought there'd be dozens of us."

"Oh, no, we're not prepared for that!" Bonnie's misty-grey eyes widened in alarm. "Even before, we'd never open this early."

"What do you mean 'before'?" Charley asked.

"The resort hasn't been open since the summer of '39. There was the war, of course, and by the time it was over, Mr. Bennett had become too ill to even contemplate it. Now he's passed Mr. Foster wants to start up again. That's why he called Carl—that's my husband—and me."

"So, you used to work here?" Freddie asked.

"Yes, since I was a young girl. Got my start as a server at fourteen and worked up to head of staff." She glanced around wistfully. "You should have seen her at her finest. Bennett's Family Resort was a real going concern. We'd be booked solid from the Victoria Day weekend in May right up to Thanksgiving in October. But when the war started, it was only the mister and missus who came here for the summers. No need for staff."

"When did you arrive?" Charley shoved her hands into her pockets and stomped her feet to try to keep warm.

"Just this afternoon." Bonnie looked around. "But the condition isn't so bad, is it?"

"Is there more staff?" Hal asked.

"Oh no, sir. It will be Carl and me. But don't worry. It's like riding a bicycle: once you know how, you never forget. You'll want for nought." Bonnie's attempt to infuse confidence into her statement didn't fool Charley. The worry in the woman's eyes gave her away.

"I'm sure it will be lovely." Charley smiled encouragingly. "I guess it will take a while for the furnace to heat up the building."

"Oh, there's no furnace, ma'am. No central heating at all. That's why we never opened in the winter. But each of the rooms has an electric heater and a fireplace. And we've laid in a goodly supply of wood for you."

No heat?

Freddie chuckled. "Sounds like one of Old Benny's challenges to test our mettle."

"He never was one to coddle," Hal agreed.

Charley turned to the two men. "It's April. It's Canada. I'm not sure a space heater and a few logs are going to cut it."

"Now, now, now, I know you're made of stronger stuff." Freddie put his arm around her. "Besides, nothing like a little chill in the air to give old Hal, here, the opportunity to chivalrously offer to help keep you warm."

"I'm game," Hal agreed, a little too eagerly.

"Some chaperone you are," Charley whispered harshly and pushed away from her brother. She glanced anxiously at Bonnie, hoping they hadn't given her the wrong impression about her relationship with Hal.

"Carl's gone through and cleaned all the fireplaces we'll be needing, and the flues, too. Once they've had a chance to get going, they'll take a lot of the dampness out of the air," Bonnie continued as if she hadn't been interrupted by their silliness.

"There, you see? It will be like Outdoor Club all over again," Freddie said.

"I knew there was a reason I wasn't in Outdoor Club," Charley countered.

"You mean in addition to it being for boys only?" Hal cocked an eyebrow.

"Oh, that wouldn't have stopped her. My sister can be quite mulish when she sets her mind to something. Theo and I spent the entirety of our childhood devising ways to escape her machinations."

"Are the fireplaces in the room already stoked?" Charley asked Bonnie.

"Oh yes, ma'am. Should be good and toasty by the time you retire. But you might like to join the others in the lounge first. It's quite warm in there already. I've laid out an assortment of biscuits, tea, and coffee. And hard liquor, too, if you'd like it." She came around the reception desk. "You can leave your luggage here; I'll see it's taken to your rooms and unpacked for you."

"I'll take my own up, thanks," Freddie said. "You two go ahead. I'll be down in a jiffy."

Charley's heart tumbled with unease as she watched Freddie disappear through the swinging door to the stairwell clutching his suitcase.

"Shall we?" Hal touched her elbow.

She took his arm and forced a smile. "We shall."

“Hal Overstreet! Is that you?” A voice boomed as they entered the lounge.

Hal propelled Charley toward a man and woman across the room. “It’s great to see you, Ralph,” he said shaking the man’s hand. “And you must be Pamela. I don’t believe we’ve had the pleasure.” He turned to Charley. “Charley, this is Ralph and Pamela Carmichael. You might not remember Ralph from school. He was in my year. Ralph, Pamela, this is Charlotte Hall, she’s Freddie Stormont’s sister.”

“Charley, please,” she said, shaking hands with the couple.

“Charley Hall, the reporter?” Pamela asked. She was about Charley’s age, with a short, stylish blonde bob and big sapphire-blue eyes. Her husband was also blond-haired and blue-eyed. They were dressed in matching ivory-coloured cable-knit sweaters and brown tweed pants.

"I thought Charley Hall was a man." Ralph's voice seemed to have one volume—loud. "That'll teach me."

"It's a common misconception," Charley said, returning his grin.

"I've been reading you for years," Pamela said. "I am thrilled to meet you in person."

"That's very kind of you." Charley could feel the heat rushing to her cheeks. She was never comfortable with such fervent praise.

"Warm?" Hal asked her, mistaking the reason for her flush. "Bonnie was right about that fire. Here, let me take your coat."

She allowed him to lift it off her shoulders and place it, along with his own, on the pile of outerwear that lay across the arm of the sofa. He returned carrying two cups of tea.

"What do you do?" Charley asked Ralph.

"He's a veterinarian," Pamela answered for her husband.

"Large breed. Farm animals mostly. No kitty-cats or puppy-dogs, sorry," Ralph added quickly, obviously used to people trying to get free advice from him.

“No need to worry about me. No pets. Never have had.”

“Never?” Hal stared at her as if she’d arrived from outer space.

She shook her head.

“That’s a real shame,” Hal said. “You’ve missed out on a big part of life.”

She didn’t feel like she’d missed out. She liked animals, but the thought of owning one had never occurred to her.

“Pet ownership is a big responsibility,” Ralph said. “One that not enough people take seriously. That’s why there are far too many strays around.”

“Growing up we always had a dog,” Hal added. “I can’t imagine a better way to teach children responsibility.”

Charley remembered some of the Overstreets’ dogs, but she had no recollection of either Hal or Poppy taking care of them. It was always Mrs. Rinehart, their former housekeeper, feeding, walking, and chasing after them when they misbehaved. It made her wonder what type of responsibility Hal had learned and whether it extended to the raising of children, too.

"I don't think I've seen you since Gavin's wedding." Ralph's change of subject was a relief to Charley.

Hal looked as if he wanted to pursue her lack of pet ownership, but instead, he raised his teacup. "To Gavin, may he rest in peace."

"To Gavin." Ralph gently tapped his teacup against Hal's and then added for Pamela and Charley's benefit, "Gavin was another friend from high school. He died in '44, Juno Beach."

"You were at Juno Beach," Pamela whispered, placing her hand on her husband's arm.

"I was one of the lucky ones." He nodded toward Hal. "You were part of the invasion, too, weren't you?"

"Parachute regiment. We were dropped behind enemy lines to neutralize Hitler's strongholds in preparation for you lot."

Ralph held out his cup. "We knew them,

we mourn them, and they will never be forgotten."

"To our fallen comrades!" Hal clinked his teacup with Ralph's again.

"We are forever grateful for their sacrifice," Charley said remembering Theo as she tapped her teacup against theirs.

"And for those made by their families and loved ones." Pamela raised her cup to join the toast.

They stood in silent contemplation until startled by a shout from across the room.

"There's the man!"

Charley turned to see two men and a woman greeting Freddie. Her heart sank a little as she noticed the three had opted for hard liquor rather than tea, and she steeled herself to not interfere if Freddie chose to join them.

"I see Bob and Sam made the cut," Hal said. "I don't recognize that young woman, though."

Charley didn't recognize the men, but that didn't surprise her. Aside from Theo, she'd never bothered with any of Freddie's friends.

Or perhaps, it was the other way around. Two years her senior, Freddie's friends never bothered with her. Only Theo had deigned to allow his best friend's little sister to occasionally tag along.

The woman was interesting, though. She was slim with a head of shiny black hair parted at the side and styled in the modern pageboy cut. She wore heavy makeup, perhaps in the mistaken assumption it would hide her youth. Charley would be surprised if she was old enough to be drinking what was in her glass. *And what is she wearing?* The burgundy silk dress would have been lovely for cocktails in Gran's drawing room, but not for hot drinks to warm up in the lounge of a family resort. She'd have to ask Freddie about her.

In another corner of the room, Charley spotted Dan and Meredith. "I'm going to go say hello to Dan Cannon and his wife," she said, excusing herself.

As she approached, she noted the couple was engaged in conversation with an older man, seated in an armchair. Although he no longer sported his trademark beard, Charley assumed the man with the wispy grey hair and round spectacles enlarging his owl-like eyes was Foster Bennett, their host. She hesitated to interrupt the trio and wondered if Freddie would mind if she joined his group instead.

"Hello, Mrs. Hall—Charley, I mean."

She recognized the slightly accented voice behind her and took a calming breath before she turned toward it. "Colin," she said, greeting the man who held the reins as Dan's biggest political backer and campaign manager. "I'm surprised to see you here. Are you hoping to drum up more support for Dan's nomination? Perhaps try to convince Hal to step down?"

His smile looked as forced as hers felt. "No, this is purely a social visit. No politics involved."

"You must be disappointed that Dan didn't get the party's nomination, though." She didn't know why she was needling him. Charley didn't like or trust Colin Banks, but they'd agreed to a truce—for Dan's sake—

some months ago. She knew it was too much to hope that with Dan's political aspirations dashed, Colin would disappear from their lives. After all, he was Meredith's brother.

"You should ask Dan about that. Although, I do have to wonder about your loyalty to our good friend. Is it your intention to rub his nose in his defeat by arriving on the arm of his political rival?"

"It's not like that. Dan knows Hal and I are old friends. I had no idea he was even going to be here."

Colin's eyes narrowed. "If you say so."

Charley opened her mouth to argue her point but was cut off by Foster Bennett clearing his throat as he rose to his feet. She turned her back on Colin and nodded a silent greeting to Dan and Meredith as they approached her.

"Greetings to you all and welcome to the Bennett Family Resort. I am sorry I haven't yet greeted each of you individually, but I promise I will make it up to you tomorrow. Right now, 'To all, to each, a fair good-night, and pleasing dreams, and slumbers light.'" He waved his arm and bowed deeply before turning on his heel and marching from the room.

“Well, that was rather abrupt but very typical for Old Benny, wouldn’t you say, Cannon?” Hal had joined their group. “Who was that he quoted? Walter Scott, I think.” He turned his back on Dan. “Meredith, it is lovely to see you again. My stomach still rumbles with pleasure whenever I remember that delicious onion tart you served at dinner a few months ago.”

“Thank you.” Meredith beamed at him. “Mrs. Harper, our housekeeper, is a genius in the kitchen.”

“You are fortunate, indeed,” Hal said.

“I didn’t expect you to be here,” Charley whispered to Dan while Hal and Meredith continued to exchange pleasantries.

“Why ever not?”

“You never had Mr. Bennett for English class.”

“Neither did you and yet, here you are.”

“I’m here as a guest of Hal’s. And Freddie’s,” she added quickly.

Dan quirked an amused eyebrow at her. "Let me guess: Freddie is supposed to be some sort of chaperone to appease your grandmother?"

"Something like that." She scowled at him and then softened her glare. "I'm sorry you didn't get the party's nomination to run for Parliament in the next election. I didn't come with Hal to tweak your nose over it."

Dan blinked several times and shook his head slightly. "The thought never occurred to me." He frowned. "It's politics, Charley. You know nothing is certain. Besides, it's probably better that I spend a few more years as an alderman anyway. Although...." He cocked his head and grinned. "I may consider throwing in my hat for the next provincial election if I get the opportunity. I'd love to kick those Tories out of the legislature."

His expression turned serious again and he took Charley's arm to draw her away from the group. "Look, I know I have no right to interfere in your love life—"

"It's not like that!"

"Be that as it may, but as your friend—as

someone who cares very much about you—please be careful of Hal Overstreet."

"Careful of Hal? Why? What—"

Hal and Meredith had stopped their conversation and were looking curiously in their direction.

"Trust me," Dan whispered before returning to his wife.

Baffled, Charley glanced around the room, her gaze settling on Freddie. She was relieved to see him holding a teacup. He looked up, as if sensing her scrutiny, made a comment to his friends and came over to her group. "Charley says you never had Old Benny as a teacher, Cannon. How'd you snag an invite?" he asked after properly greeting Meredith and Colin.

"Isn't it obvious? Have you not noticed who's here?" Dan used his hand to gesture to all the guests in the room. When neither Freddie nor Hal seemed to comprehend his meaning, he expelled a breath of frustration. "It's fifteen years, almost to the weekend."

"I'm sorry, Pal, but I don't—" Hal began.

"Wait! Wait! Wait!" Freddie said. "The spring camp. Is that what you're getting at?"

"Is that right?" Hal cocked his head. "How the devil did you remember that, Freddie?" He glanced back to Dan. "That's an interesting connection, Cannon."

"I don't understand," Charley said. "Was this some kind of Outdoor Club thing? I didn't think you did Outdoor Club, Dan."

"It was the spring of our grade 9 year." He turned to Hal. "It was the only camp I went to and I remember it well. Everyone in this room was there. And the ones who aren't...."

"Are dead," Hal said. "Gavin, Theo. Who else was there?"

"There were ten in total. Only seven of us are still alive," Dan said. "Paul Logan died in the Italian campaign."

Charley gazed around the room, counting the men in her head: Freddie, Hal, Dan, Ralph, Bob and Sam. "There's only six here."

Dan nodded solemnly. "I can't imagine Elliot Shaw coming. That's what I was asking Foster about. He wouldn't say one way or another, but I wouldn't blame Shaw for refusing, after everything that happened."

"I don't remember Shaw," Hal said slowly. "Frankly, Cannon, I don't recall you ever coming to camp."

"Elliot and I were tenderfoots," Dan said. "We both only went that one time."

"What happened to Elliot that you think he wouldn't want to come?" Charley turned to Freddie. "Do you remember him?"

"I know what happened to him, but that was later. Theo and I spent most of the spring camp on our own adventure, away from the group." Freddie turned to Dan. "Are you saying what happened to Shaw...?"

"Was directly related to the spring camp?" Dan hadn't taken his eyes off Hal. "Yes."

"Why don't you say what's on your mind?" Hal sounded annoyed.

"Okay, I will. A few days after we got back from the camp, Elliot Shaw tried to kill himself." Dan turned to Charley. "You don't remember him at all?"

She shook her head. "I spent most of my

time with Poppy and the other girls. Was he with us in elementary school?"

"No, his family moved to Kingston partway through our grade 9 year. He'd only been at Kingston Collegiate a few months."

"And why do you blame the spring camp?" Hal had squared his shoulders and puffed out his chest. "He sounds like he already had his own troubles. New town. New school."

"You don't get it, Overstreet, do you? Maybe it was nothing to you and Ralph and Gavin... I suppose you treated all the tenderfoots the same way. Belittling and tormenting us. Making us undergo ridiculous —dangerous—initiation rites."

"It was only a little teasing," Hal said with a shrug. "Everyone did it. Built character. Made you feel like you earned your place in the group."

"Except it wasn't *'only a little teasing,'* was it?" Dan shot back. "You did everything you could think of to embarrass and humiliate us. Elliot couldn't take it. He was afraid to return to school. Afraid you'd tell everyone how you scared him so badly he wet his pants and spent the night crying into his pillow."

Charley wasn't surprised by the passion she heard in Dan's voice. He harboured a hero complex, always ready to defend the underdog, but never more so than when it came to hazing. He'd even gone so far as to get a coach fired for allowing it to happen to a rookie member of his university's rowing team.

"What is this really about?" Hal asked, his tone challenging. "Is it sour grapes for losing the party's nomination? Frankly, I expected better from you, Cannon." He turned to Charley and held out his hand, motioning for her to take it. "Charley, are you coming?"

She crossed her arms over her chest. "In a moment." She turned back to Dan. "You said he tried to kill himself. I take it he wasn't successful. Do you know what happened to him? Did Elliot ever come back to school?"

"I believe he was in the hospital for a few months and planned to transfer to another school in the fall. Unfortunately, his parents were both killed in a car accident that summer and he was sent to Toronto to live with relatives. That's all I know."

"Charley!"

She winced at Hal's sharp command. She'd have to talk to him about his tone. She wasn't a dog to be ordered about. But he was also her date for the week and she couldn't very well ignore him.

"It's almost time for the eclipse," Freddie announced. "Hey, everyone, if you want to see a spectacular sight, grab your coat and come outside."

Charley gave Freddie a thankful smile for changing the topic and went to retrieve her coat from the pile. Hal was already standing at the door to the lounge. She took his arm and allowed him to lead her back through the reception area and out onto the front deck.

As she watched the earth's shadow slowly erase the full moon, she tried unsuccessfully to imagine the man standing beside her as a bully. Hal had always been so warm and caring, never complaining when he was called upon to look after her and Poppy when they were younger. He'd led men into battle and was a decorated war hero.

But Dan's warning....

Could Hal be right? Was Dan being a poor sport after losing the nomination? Even though Dan downplayed his disappointment, she knew how much he wanted to be a federal candidate. Heck, he even got married for it.

She glanced over her shoulder, noting that only Dan and Meredith hadn't joined the rest of the guests outside.

Still, it was odd that of all the students Foster Bennett had taught over the years, it was only these six men who'd been invited for the week. Dan's theory would explain why he was included.

But not why he accepted.

Charley looked around the dining room. Six tables, each with the capacity of seating up to eight people, were arrayed around the empty room.

"Good morning, Mrs. Hall," Bonnie said hipping open the swinging door between the kitchen and the dining room. Relieved of her toque and heavy coat, the woman was likely in her mid-forties, Charley guessed. She had a pleasant, round face surrounded by a mass of red curls. The sleeves of her brown cotton blouse were pulled up above her elbows to reveal lean, well-muscled arms. Thankfully she was also carrying a large silver pot. "Coffee?"

"You're a lifesaver." Charley smiled at her and sat down at the nearest table. "Am I the last one up?" She had a tough time falling asleep and when she finally did, it was far from restful. She awoke at her usual seven o'clock but decided to take advantage of the fact she was on holiday and huddled back under the covers, hoping to catch a few more minutes of slumber. She was surprised to discover it was close to ten a.m. when she next looked at the clock on the nightstand.

"Oh, no. They've been straggling in all morning. There's still a few that haven't come down yet." Bonnie turned over a white ceramic mug and began pouring. "There's milk and sugar on the sideboard. Shall I bring some over for you?"

"No, thank you. Black is fine." Charley picked up the mug and inhaled the deep, rich aroma. She took a sip and sighed. Good, strong coffee, just the way she liked it.

"Can I get you some eggs or porridge? I think you'll find the fresh air will give you quite an appetite."

"Eggs and toast would be lovely."

"There she is!" Freddie bounded into the dining room, his cheeks flushed from being outside. He shed his coat and sat down in the chair beside her. "*Brrr*, there's a definite chill in the air. I think the temperature's dropping," he said, vigorously rubbing his hands together.

"There's a storm moving in, for sure," Bonnie said, re-emerging from the kitchen with the coffee pot. She poured a mug for Freddie and then noticing Charley's was empty, refilled hers, too. "I'll leave it here, shall I?" she said, placing the coffee pot on the table.

"That might be for the best," Freddie agreed. "And can I have another plate of eggs?"

"Another?" Charley eyed her brother. "How long have you been up?"

"Long enough to go for a walk by the lake and scout out what Benny has planned for us today."

The door from the kitchen swung open again and an enormous man appeared carrying an equally enormous armload of cut logs. He nodded to them and proceeded to re-arrange the pile of wood stacked along the outside wall. Bonnie had been right last night. Between the well-stoked fireplaces and electric heaters, the individual rooms in the resort were toasty warm. The hallways, however, were another matter.

The man rose and stretched out a kink in his shoulder, straining the blue plaid shirt he was wearing. Charley had to crane her neck to look up at him. Even in the high-ceilinged dining room, he seemed huge. He had to be six-foot-seven, at least.

"You must be Mister Freddie's sister. I'm Carl." He gave her a broad smile.

"Good to meet you, Carl. I'm Charley." She tilted her head way back so she could smile up at him.

"Oh no, ma'am. It's one thing to refer to the chaps by their first names, but the Bennetts would never allow me to do so with the ladies. You'll be Mrs. Hall while you're here." He tapped his fingers to the side of his forehead in a salute and turned to help Bonnie who'd come into the room balancing four plates along her arms, and a basket of jams in one hand.

"You're getting a late start, aren't you?"

Freddie asked, digging into his eggs once they were alone.

"I had trouble falling asleep." She poked at her plate and then opened the jar of marmalade and began to spread some onto a piece of toast she still hadn't decided she was going to eat. "I keep thinking about what Dan said last night. Do you think it's true?"

"That this is some sort of reunion of everyone who was at spring camp?" Freddie chewed thoughtfully. "It's turned out to be. But whether that was the intention..." He shrugged. "I can't think of another time we were all together."

"You were very quick to pick up on Dan's hint about the significance of who all is here." She leaned forward. "Is it because you remember what happened to him and Elliot?"

"No, no, no," he replied quickly. "As I said last night, I don't remember much about what happened with the group. Theo and I were off on our own pretty much that whole weekend."

"But you said you knew what happened to Elliot Shaw afterwards."

"That he tried to kill himself?" Freddie

picked up the silver pot to top up their coffees. "I remember there were rumours at the time. There always are when a new kid's involved. But I also heard he contracted polio and that was why he left school."

"Why don't I have any memory of this? Dan says he was in our grade."

Freddie set down his fork. "Look, Charley, memory is a funny thing. You are certain something happened one way but when you talk to someone else who was there, they recall it as something completely different. There are things you think you'll remember your entire life and the memory fades away, while other things you try to forget stay with you forever."

She reached out and squeezed his hand. It always came back to the war for him: Theo's death on the beach at Dieppe and his own years as a prisoner of war.

"I remember his parents dying, though." He gave her a rueful smile. "But the rumour was he killed them and was sent to either Rockwood Asylum or Kingston Pen—take your pick."

"That's crazy!"

"Sure, it is." He leaned back and frowned. "What is it you're concerned about? Is it what happened to Elliot Shaw? Or is it that Hal may not be the man you think he is?"

"Isn't it the same? One proves the other."

Freddie shrugged. "Maybe. But you're a good judge of character. What do *you* think?"

She gave up any pretence of eating. Ruminating about what might have happened at that spring camp was precisely what had kept her up most of the night. She'd known both Dan and Hal for years. Maybe it was nothing more than a political rivalry between the two men—but she still found it difficult to believe that her best friend would be willing to stoop so low as to attack another man's reputation to score political points.

Unless it wasn't politics at all. Maybe it was personal. Maybe it was her.

No.

She pushed that thought away. Dan had made his decision, or more accurately—according to him—Charley had made it for him by rebuffing his marriage proposals. He was now wed to Meredith and they seemed well-suited. Charley didn't know why she was finding it so hard to let go of her infatuation with him once and for all.

"I can see this is gnawing at you," Freddie said. "My suggestion is to forget about it for the week. Then, if it's still bugging you when you get home, ask Grace to dig out the newspapers from 1934 to see if Shaw's parents really did die in a car accident. She may also be able to find out if and why he was hospitalized that spring."

He stood up and slipped on his coat. "I think you need some fresh air. I got Carl to spill the beans on what Benny has planned for us this week. It's going to be a series of outdoor competitions. I'm confident in my fire-starting, tracking, and shelter-building skills, but I need to work on my archery. Come with me. Shooting a bow and arrow will help take your mind off your troubles. I guarantee it."

Charley smiled up at her brother. "Thanks, but I think I'm going to find a good book and sit by the fire for a bit. I expect once the competition starts, we'll be expected to remain outside for hours on end, and that will be enough fresh air for me."

Freddie *tsked*, then gave her shoulder an affectionate squeeze and exited the dining room.

Grace. Why hadn't she thought of her?

Charley couldn't—or didn't want to—wait until she got home to learn the truth about Elliot Shaw and his parents. She finished the rest of her coffee and strode out of the dining room.

In the reception area, she found the telephone behind the main counter and wrote down her name and the number she was calling on the notepad beside it so the resort could charge her for the long-distance fee. Then she dialled the number of the *Kingston Tribune*'s archives.

Grace answered on the first ring. "Well, I didn't expect to be hearing from you," she said. "You're supposed to be on holiday. It's too bad you didn't call a little earlier. You just missed Mark."

"Why was Mark there?" Charley couldn't

imagine why the private detective would be visiting the *Trib*.

"Looking for you, of course."

"Is he working on a case?"

Even through the phone line, Charley could detect Grace's huff of exasperation. Grace had made it plain she was certain Mark Spadina was romantically interested in Charley, but Charley had her doubts. Mark was far more likely to condemn than compliment her, and he only ever called when there was a murder to solve.

"He wanted to let you know that he's going out of town for the Easter weekend, in case you needed him for anything."

"Where's he going?" The question was out before she could stop herself. She winced, knowing it would only encourage Grace's matchmaking.

"Toronto. He's helping out at the orphanage, organizing Easter egg hunts and such while educating the children on the need to stick to the 'straight and narrow,' he says." Grace giggled at her attempt to imitate his stern tone. "He dropped off some chocolates; said he'd bought too many and the sisters would have his hide for spoiling the kids. But that was an excuse to bring you a present. Too bad you're not here. I guess I will have to enjoy them for you."

"Chocolate will keep," Charley said, trying to imagine Mark playing with a bunch of children. Not for the first time she found herself wondering about his life away from Kingston. She knew very little about the former police detective—only that he was born to a prostitute in the Don Jail and was raised in a religious orphanage. And he was Dan's half-brother.

"These won't. Sorry." Grace's voice was muffled, no doubt by one of Charley's chocolates. "Now, what do you need?"

Charley could hear the scratching of Grace's pencil taking notes as she summarized what she was looking for.

"Okay, got it. I don't know how fast I'll be able to get the information to you. Tomorrow is Good Friday, and everything is pretty much closed for the holiday weekend. But I'll see what I can do. When are you back?"

"Tuesday." Charley thanked her friend and hung up.

What now?

She could join Freddie on the archery range. He was right: the cool, brisk air would probably help her feel more invigorated. As if in warning, the wind rattled the windowpane and a whoosh of cold air rushed in through the plank walls. She dismissed the idea. She didn't feel like going out in the cold yet.

She wandered into the lounge and immediately regretted her decision.

"Charley, your ears must be burning," Meredith said, waving her over.

Charley hesitated. She didn't dislike Dan's wife. In fact, it was very hard to find things about the woman to dislike. Meredith was poised and self-assured. She was well-educated and kind.

But...

There was something about her that Charley hadn't been able to warm up to. It wasn't simply that she'd married Dan, although she'd be lying to herself if she pretended that wasn't part of it. Meredith said and did all the right things, but she didn't seem to have any real personality of her own.

Meredith Banks Cannon was a chameleon and Charley couldn't quite make out her true colours.

Fortunately, she wasn't alone. Pamela Carmichael was sitting in the armchair across from Meredith, so Charley pasted a smile on her face and went to join them.

"I was just telling Meredith how excited I was to meet you last night," Pamela said. "I'm so sorry Ralph said he'd thought you were a man. I gave him what for when we went back to our room."

"Oh, don't worry about that. He's hardly the first person to do so," Charley said. "I decided to use Charley rather than Charlotte so I wouldn't immediately be dismissed for being female."

"It's rather unfortunate that you had to. Charlotte is a beautiful name." Pamela beamed at her.

"But Charley better suits you," Meredith said.

"Has anyone seen Sam?" Charley

recognized the young woman with the inappropriate outfit from last night poking her head into the lounge. The flouncy lime green chiffon dress and multi-coloured high heels she had on today were equally impractical for the frosty resort. Charley glanced at both Meredith and Pamela. All three of them had chosen patterned thick wool sweaters, twill pants and leather boots.

"Sorry, Trixie, we haven't seen him." Pamela's tone was brusque.

Trixie turned around several times, looking into the reception area and back at the women. After a few twirls, she shrugged her shoulders and bounded away.

Pamela leaned forward and whispered, "Sam Winn brought her here as his date. Can you imagine? To a *family* resort?"

"What's wrong with that?" Charley asked. "I came as Hal's date."

"Oh, it's not the same thing at all," Pamela countered. "They're sharing a room. And Ralph tells me Sam is already married. It's obvious she's his *mistress*. Frankly, it's an insult to the rest of us." Pamela clicked her tongue and raised her hands in mock horror.

Oh, dear, Pamela Carmichael was one of *those* people. Whenever Charley encountered a gossip, she could hear Gran's disapproval ringing in her ears, usually citing a favourite quote from Eleanor Roosevelt: *Great minds discuss ideas. Average minds discuss events. Small minds discuss people.*

Charley glanced at Meredith to see if she shared Pamela's opinion, but Dan's wife wasn't paying attention to her. She was, instead, staring past them, her eyes round and her mouth formed in a perfect "O". Charley swivelled in her chair to see what had startled her so.

A man was standing in the doorway right where Trixie had been. He'd obviously just arrived as he was still wearing a black overcoat with a red scarf wrapped around his neck and a black felt pilgrim hat. A thin, black moustache looked as if it had been drawn over his lip. In one hand he held a burgundy leather suitcase, in the other a smouldering pipe.

"Good morning, ladies. I am wondering if you could direct me to whoever is in charge of assigning rooms. I'm afraid I'm a little late arriving."

"And you are?" Pamela asked.

"Oh, my apologies. Forgive my terrible manners." He set down his suitcase and doffed his hat. "I'm Elliot Shaw."

Although it was still early in the season, the weather had been so sunny and warm the past few days Charley had allowed herself to be lulled into believing that winter was good and truly gone. Now, the sky was an ominous grey and a damp wind was blowing across the lake. At least she'd had the foresight to pack that thick wool sweater and pair of extra warm socks, although now she was wondering if they were going to be enough this week.

"There'll be a biting wind down by the lake, you wait and see," Bonnie warned as she stood at the exit inspecting each of the women's outerwear before allowing them to join the men. She'd insisted Charley take a second scarf while Trixie was given a full wardrobe change from Bonnie's own closet.

Charley stomped the ground and rubbed

her hands together. She desperately wanted to go back inside. Unfortunately, there was an overabundance of male bravado on display, which seemed to have infected the women, too. She'd thought—hoped, really—that Trixie would have succumbed an hour ago. Charley refused to be the first to break.

Of course, the men weren't standing around like they were, and all that activity was keeping them warm enough. Although he hadn't been a member of the Outdoor Club, Colin was included in the competition. She didn't know whether to be relieved or irritated that Foster hadn't extended an invitation to the women, too.

She still didn't know why Colin was there at all. He and Meredith had lived in Kingston for several years. Didn't he have friends other than his sister and her new husband? Wherever Meredith and Dan went, Colin was sure to be found tagging along.

Charley watched the lake's shore where the eight men were crouched low, foreheads creased in concentration as each tried to be the first to start a fire with nothing more than sticks, and then to nurse it with small twigs or whatever they could find until the flame grew large enough to burn through a line of twine that had been strung across their small pits. She tried to edge close, hoping to warm herself on the struggling flames, but had been shooed away.

This was the third challenge of the day, and while most of the men had taken a light-hearted approach to the competition, the rivalry between Hal and Dan had ratcheted up with each event.

Hal won the shelter-building competition, completing his structure only moments before Dan. In the second event, tracking, Dan finished first by a formidable margin, although Hal downplayed the relevance of timing in his second-place finish.

Both Hal and Dan were nursing small flames. Only two other men had managed to get their fires started: Freddie and Elliot Shaw.

Charley kept a close eye on Elliot since his arrival, but the man seemed to harbour no ill-will toward any of his former Outdoor Club comrades. He'd greeted them all affably and had willingly taken part in the activities, adopting a self-deprecating demeanour when he finished close to the bottom of the pack each time.

He was a slim, wiry man, not too tall—slightly shorter than Charley's five-foot-seven, and wore his dark hair slicked back from his face. He must have known what was coming when he accepted Foster's invitation and had made sure he was dressed to spend hours outside in inclement weather. She spotted the Eaton's sales tag hanging from the pocket of his navy-blue parka.

A frosty droplet landed on Charley's eyelash, blurring her view. She wiped it away with the back of her mitten and glanced up. An icy dart landed between her eyes.

"Is it raining?" she called to Foster. How could that be? It had to be below freezing.

Foster removed a leather glove and held out his hand. "Guess so." He turned back to the beach, unconcerned—probably because he was wearing a long waxed cotton coat that would repel any precipitation.

Charley had been surprised by the teacher's attitude throughout the competition. He goaded rather than encouraged, deliberately heightening the tension between the contestants. The rivalry between Hal and Dan seemed to especially delight him.

Maybe that was his way of pushing them to do their best. She remembered Freddie's baseball coach yelling at him for not catching a fly ball when he was just a young boy. And Dan was always grumbling about the unrealistic demands of his coach when he rowed for the university team. Despite their tough coaches, both men had stuck with their sports for years.

Charley could feel the rain now, not the patter of gentle droplets but the thud of heavy globules. She scooted over to where Foster was standing. "I guess we'll have to postpone the archery," she suggested hopefully.

"Why would we do that?" His eyebrows knitted together as he shot her a look before resuming his observation of the competition. "That's the problem with you city folk. Go inside if you want, but these boys are tough. A little rain's not going to scare them off."

"I think you'll find I'm no shrinking violet, either." Charley bristled. He said "city folk" but she was quite certain it was a dig at her gender. Outdoor Club had always been, and was still, boys only.

"Charley Hall. I know who you are." He turned to face her. "I've read your articles in the *Kingston Tribune*."

"And?"

"Well, it's not literature, now, is it? Maybe if you'd been in my class, you'd have pursued a different path. There are some wonderful lady novelists I could have pointed you toward."

"Are you saying Mr. Littlestone and the rest of KCI's English department failed me?" *Lady novelists?* The only female writer she'd ever studied in high school was the poet Elizabeth Barrett Browning.

"Littlestone?"

"Yes, Mr. Littlestone. I went to Kingston Collegiate, too, you know. While it's true, I never had you as a teacher, I'm sure, as you were head of the English department, you made certain the other teachers were up to the job."

Foster's lips pursed and he cocked his head as his eyes bored into hers, the only part of her face that was visible between the two scarfs she'd wrapped around her head. She let him stew for a couple more seconds and then admitted, "Hall is my married name. You would have known me as Charlotte Stormont."

"Freddie's sister." He nodded, satisfied.

"Yes. Did he tell you he's to have two of his poems published? I am sure that should satisfy you since you actually did have him as a student."

"Is he now?" Foster grinned.

He should have kept the beard, Charley thought. It hid his weak chin and thin lips.

"I win!"

Her gaze snapped back to the beach where Freddie was standing, his arms raised in victory.

"Oh, well done." Charley applauded loudly, as much in relief that she didn't have to feign happiness or commiseration for Hal or Dan as in real pleasure at Freddie's success.

A loud rumble rolled along the lake and the heavens opened up to douse the meagre fires in an icy shower.

Charley smiled beneath her scarf as the eight men scrambled past her to seek refuge under the tin roof of the resort's lodge.

"Dinner was wonderful," Charley said to Bonnie who was refilling her teacup.

Bonnie's face lit up with the compliment. "I'm glad you enjoyed it. I know it was just beef stew, but it's been a while since I've cooked for so many, and I was worried we'd have either too much or too little."

"Well, you got it just right."

Bonnie thanked her and then hurried over to where Sam was waving an empty wine glass to get her attention. Sam, Trixie, and Bob were the only guests who'd taken up Foster's offer of wine with dinner. Although the dessert dishes had been cleared away and everyone else was sipping tea, Sam had pressed his host to open another bottle of pinot.

It had been an interesting evening, full of small talk and catching up on what people were doing now. Vacation or not, Charley couldn't switch off her curious reporter nature as she listened intently to the conversation. Sam Winn worked on the assembly line at General Motors in Oshawa. Trixie—Sam had never actually introduced her, so no one knew her last name—was a secretary there. Bob Barryman had married his high school sweetheart and become a teacher, which of course made Foster chortle with glee.

"Nancy would have loved to come," Bob said, "but with our three little ones, she couldn't get away."

Charley remembered Nancy. She'd been in her year. A bright student. Very quiet, though. Kept to herself mostly—at least that was Charley's memory of her from high school. But in elementary school, she'd been more outgoing, hadn't she? Maybe she was thinking of a different Nancy. Freddie was right, memory was a funny thing.

The tables had been pushed together for the meal so they could all sit together in two long rows. Charley had managed to place herself directly across from Elliot Shaw, who'd taken the seat to the right of Foster at the head of the table. It was a bit awkward because it put her between Foster and Dan, moving Meredith to her husband's other side and leaving Hal to sit across the table, between Elliot and Freddie.

Elliot was personable and showed an interest in what everyone—including the women—had to say. However, he said little about himself until Charley asked him directly, and then all she managed to find out was that he was unmarried and worked in a shoe store in Toronto.

As the rising wind rattled the windowpanes and the room grew dim in the twilight, a solemness settled over the table and talk turned to the war. Charley was fascinated and horrified in equal measure as she listened intently to the stories rarely shared in the presence of those who'd not been there. Stories told not to one-up each other, but in reverence for their collective experience and remembrance of those who hadn't come home.

Ralph and Bob traded stories about their time in the infantry and how they'd been frustrated when the invasion into Normandy had to be delayed by a day due to the weather. They compared their feelings of seasickness during the rough Channel crossing, and their terror from the noise of battle when they came ashore.

Sam claimed responsibility for much of that noise as he'd been a gunner in the nose of one of the Lancaster bombers sent over to "soften up" the beach defences.

Colin talked about his clandestine activities with the French Resistance. Charley noted that he omitted the part about how he'd left South Africa with a fortune in diamonds from his fascist-sympathizing father meant to help the Nazis, but that he gave to the Allies instead.

Then Foster told of his time in the futile

trenches of the Somme during the Great War: the hellish conditions of soldiers being crammed together in the cold, damp underground, and their constant fear of mustard gas.

"What about the other story?" Sam yelled from the far end of the table.

"Oh? What story is that?" Foster asked.

"You know, the one about how you fought hand-to-hand against the Fritz and st-stabbed him with his own d-d-dagger." Sam was starting to slur his words.

"You still remember that?"

"We sure do," Ralph chimed in. "You'd recite it every campfire. Sam's right, it wouldn't feel proper for us all to be here and not have you tell it."

"I remember that dagger," Hal said. "The top boy at each camp was given the honour of holding onto it until the next camp," he added for Charley's benefit. "How we all coveted it."

"Yeah, but it always went to Gavin, remember?" Ralph said. "Do you still have it, Benny? I remember at some point you stopped handing it out."

Foster shrugged. "I probably got tired of always giving it to Gavin. It's likely tucked away in a drawer somewhere. I haven't thought about it in years."

"Well, at least you can tell us the story," Ralph insisted.

"Yeah, how 'bout it, for old time's sh–sake," Sam persisted.

Foster rubbed his chin. "It's been a while, but I guess I remember it all right."

Charley glanced down the table as the men sat forward anxiously awaiting the tale. Everyone except Freddie, who stared down into his cup, his fingers fiddling with the teaspoon. His face was pale with bright red splotches suffusing his cheeks, a sure sign of his agitation.

She'd noticed he'd gone quiet when the war tales had begun—keeping his own stories to himself. No one else had spent the war in a German POW camp. There was no camaraderie for what he'd experienced.

Foster's story seemed a bit anti-climactic after the buildup Sam and Ralph had given it, and he told it without emotion. He and another soldier had gone in search of food from a local farm and had encountered a pair of German soldiers in the barn doing the same. Too close for bayonets and unwilling to alert the farmer with gunfire, they'd fought hand-to-hand with the Canadians ultimately successful.

Charley hoped, for Freddie's sake, that Foster's tale would be the end of the stories for the evening, but as soon as he finished, Ralph called out for Hal to tell them about parachuting into France.

"C'mon, Major, no point being shy about it," Ralph bellowed from his end of the table.

Charley glared at Hal, willing him to notice her. But he'd turned toward Ralph, Bob and Sam and began to tell of how, under the cover of darkness, in the late hours of June 5, 1944, his parachute brigade took off from an airport in England and was dropped behind enemy lines. In addition to the equipment needed for their mission, all they had was an escape kit with French currency and two 24-hour ration packs. They'd been given two hours to destroy the bridges over the Dives river and hold the area for the Allies.

Charley felt helpless. She wished she could say something—do something—to stop Hal. But interrupting him would be disrespectful to the soldiers who'd risked their lives. Very few of them ever talked with their families and loved ones about what they'd experienced overseas, and she knew she should be honoured that these brave men were doing so now.

But Freddie...

She glanced at her brother. His head was down, his entire body stone-still. How much more could he take?

"I think we've told enough war stories for the night," Dan said, cutting off Hal as he was about to launch into another adventure. "Let's move on to more pleasant subjects shall we, for the sake of the ladies present."

"Bless you," she whispered to Dan under her breath. She noticed him throw a concerned glance at Freddie.

"Figures, coming from the likes of you," Hal shot back in a challenging tone. "I think you should change your shirt. You're more suited to yellow, aren't you Cannon?"

Gasps went round the table. Everyone turned to Dan.

He remained silent, but his jaw was clenched.

The heavy legs of Charley's chair scraped along the stone floor as she leapt to her feet. "That's not fair," she said, her voice shaking with emotion. "Just because Dan didn't go overseas to fight, doesn't mean he's a coward. There are other ways—"

"Charley!" Dan's reprimand cracked like a whip.

"Charley, please," Meredith hissed from the other side of her husband.

Further down the table, Colin uttered something she took to be a South African curse word.

"You mean like finishing a law degree so he can go to work in Daddy's shipyard and drink tea on Mommy's sofa?" Hal spat out scornfully. "I think every real man in this room would disagree with you, my dear."

"Charley, please sit down." Dan's voice

was quiet but firm. He tugged on her arm, pulling her back down into her chair. "I appreciate that you want to defend me, but it's not necessary. I have nothing to prove."

"That's precisely the type of response I'd expect from the likes of you," Hal said.

"Gentlemen—" Foster began but was overcome by a fit of coughing.

Elliot jumped up and began pounding on the older man's back. "Are you all right, sir?" he asked when Foster had recovered.

"I am feeling a little under the weather. Maybe I should retire and leave the rest of the evening to you young folk."

Elliot placed his palm on Foster's forehead and then pressed the back of his hand against each of his cheeks. "You don't feel flushed."

Foster was wracked by another bout of coughing. When it subsided, he gripped the edge of the table and steadied himself as he got up from his chair. "I will see you all in the morning."

Elliot's eyes followed Foster as he left the room. "I don't like the sound of that. It came on so suddenly. I'll check on him later to make sure he's okay."

"Do you have medical training?" Charley asked.

"I was an aidman during the war." He gave a small shrug. "Mostly retrieving the injured and carrying stretchers for the medics, but you pick up a thing or two."

"Can I get anyone anything else?" Bonnie bustled out from the kitchen carrying an empty tray to clear away the last of their dishes.

But everyone had had enough. The mood had been broken and it wasn't long before all had made their excuses and headed up to their rooms.

It was obvious that Hal was annoyed with her, but Charley sensed it was best to give him the night to cool down before she tried to make amends. Once she told him how the stories were affecting Freddie, he'd understand and hopefully realize he owed Dan an apology.

Freddie accompanied her to her room. Her inquiry about how he was feeling seemed to surprise him, but she knew better than to explain herself. He was a proud man who kept his demons tightly leashed.

In bed, Charley's eyes grew heavy from the hypnotic tapping of icy rain drops hitting the metal roof and she drew the covers up to her chin. She was exhausted from standing in the cold all day and the tense exchange after dinner, and so sleep found her much more easily that night.

She sat up suddenly, startled from slumber by a sharp sound. She looked around trying to get her bearings.

And then she heard it again. A cracking sound like splintering wood and then a crash of something heavy hitting the ground.

Charley glanced at the clock on her bedside table. *Six-thirty-five.*

Shards of pale pink light were slipping into her room between the misaligned slats of the window blind. She considered getting up to see what had caused all the banging, but the air in the room was frigid.

Probably Carl bringing in wood for the fireplaces. At least she hoped so.

She lay back and slowed her breathing to calm her racing heart. She snuggled beneath the covers and closed her eyes, hoping to catch a few more hours of sleep.

She'd almost drifted off when she heard the unmistakable sound of a piercing scream.

Charley was on her feet in an instant.

She pressed the switch for the lamp on the bedside table, but nothing happened. She flicked it back and forth several times. Still nothing.

The soles of her feet began to sting from the icy cold floor. She reached under her bed for her slippers and slid them on. They were cold, too, but they would soon warm up. Her housecoat lay across the end of her bed, and she shrugged into it.

She'd expected the fire to have burned itself out, but what about the electric heater? She stumbled across the dim room and held her hand in front of the heater, but there was no warmth radiating from it.

Must have lost power in the storm.

No, time to worry about that now. She opened her door and stepped into the hallway, cocking an ear but hearing nothing.

I'm positive I heard a scream. A woman's scream.

The door across from hers opened and Freddie emerged, wrapped in a blanket, his bright red hair sticking out at all angles. His eyes, however, were alert.

"You heard it too?" she asked.

He nodded.

She looked along the corridor, expecting more doors to open. "Where is everyone else? Surely, we can't be the only two."

Freddie had already started toward the stairwell. "It came from below and our rooms are closest to the stairs. The others probably didn't hear a thing. You wait here. I'll go see what's going on."

Not bloody likely.

Charley was close on his heels as Freddie bounded down the stairs to the first floor. They paused at the bottom.

"This way." Charley dodged past him,

moving toward the sounds of high-pitched gasping sobs and deep, soothing murmurs of a male voice.

They turned into the corridor that ran behind the reception area. There was a gaping hole in the wall about halfway down. As they approached, she saw shards of wood where the hinges had once hung, and a rough wooden door lying on the floor inside the room.

Carl had his tree trunk-like arms around his wife, gently stroking her hair as she cried convulsive tears. "Careful, Mrs. Hall, it's slippery right there," he warned as Charley approached.

"Oh, yes, I see it. Careful Freddie, there's a patch of ice here," Charley called over her shoulder as Freddie caught up. She stepped gingerly. "What happened? Is Bonnie all right?"

"It's not her, ma'am." Carl pointed toward the bed in the corner.

Foster Bennett was lying on his back with his arms crossed over his chest. His eyes were closed, and he looked like he was sleeping. Except that his skin had taken on an ashy colour and his hands were as blue as the woollen afghan covering him.

"Is he...?" Freddie whispered from the doorway.

Charley didn't need to feel for a pulse. The poor man was as still as a stone, and there were no puffs of condensation rising from his mouth in the icy air. "Yes. Quite dead."

"Poor bloke," Freddie said, echoing Charley's thoughts. "But at least it looks like he drifted off in his sleep."

Charley nudged Foster's elbow, but the limb wouldn't give. *Rigor mortis*, she surmised. But it could be the cold, too. "When did the power go out?" she asked.

Carl shrugged. "Can't say for sure. Sometime after midnight, anyway. Phone line's down, too."

"You tried to call the police already?" Charley asked him.

"No ma'am. I tried to contact the hydro office to tell them we was out of electricity. I'll have to make a trip into town as soon as the snow stops. A foot or more's already fallen since midnight."

Rain, snow, and now a dead body. This wasn't the relaxing vacation she'd envisioned. "You can notify the police, too," Charley said.

"Why would we need the police?" Freddie asked. "Undertaker or doctor maybe to make it official. But police?"

"A sudden unexplained death." Charley carefully pulled back the afghan and scanned the length of the body. There were no obvious signs of trauma. No gaping wounds. No blood. No ligature marks around his neck. "Asphyxiation?" she mumbled. "Pillow, maybe?"

"Do you see tiny pinpoint haemorrhages on his face?" Freddie asked from across the room.

"No, only the nicks from a razor he used to shave." She straightened, baffled. "Poison?"

She'd asked the question more as a personal musing and was surprised when Freddie answered again. "There aren't many that would work that quickly. We'd have seen some early signs yesterday if it had been poison—nausea, vomiting, nosebleed..."

"What about cyanide?" Charley asked. "That's the one they show in films. The bad guy bites down on a capsule and dies right away."

"Are his lips blue? His extremities?" Freddie asked.

"It's below freezing. Everything is blue," Charley replied.

"It's doubtful anyway. There would probably be some sign of convulsions or other distress before he died."

"How do you know all this?" Charley turned to her brother.

"From Laine's medical textbooks. After her head injury, she used to get bad headaches if she read for any length of time, so I read the books to her."

Charley remembered that time. Laine, Grace's close friend and roommate, had been a medical student when she'd been attacked and suffered a severe concussion. She'd mostly recovered, but still found the fast pace and bright lights of the emergency room too difficult to manage and had shifted her studies to pathology. “Given how squeamish you are, I’m surprised you were able to get through those textbooks.”

“Who says I’m squeamish?”

“Well, you’re the one hanging out by the door. If you’re not squeamish, why not come over here with me?”

“Hmmm.” Freddie stroked his beard and gave her a crooked smile. “I concede your point. But there’s a huge difference between reading about *subita incognita mortem* and seeing it up close.”

Charley raised her eyebrows questioning.

“Sudden unexplained death,” Freddie translated.

She glanced back at the body. *Unexplained*. She didn’t like that word. It didn’t seem right. Foster was hale and hearty last night. Well, except for that coughing fit before he retired for the evening. “Elliot said he was going to check on him. Does anyone know if he did?” She glanced between Carl and her brother.

"I'll go find out," Freddie said and darted from the room.

She turned her attention to Carl and Bonnie. Both, like Freddie, stood across the room and away from the body. "Can you tell me how you found him?" She pointed to the door lying on the floor. "You must have thought something was wrong to force the door into his room."

"I was getting ready to go out and collect more wood for the fireplaces," Carl said. "I figured we'd be needing a lot more what with the power being out."

"It was me." Bonnie stepped out of his embrace and dabbed her red eyes with a handkerchief. "I'm not usually this emotional, it's… We were so excited that Bennett's was going to open up again. These were good jobs, and it meant Carl and I wouldn't have to be sep-sep-separated…" She gulped. "Now this." She turned to her husband. "What are we going to do? I can go back to the pharmacy, but…"

"Everything will be fine." Carl's voice

sounded confident, but he seemed unable to look directly into his wife's eyes.

"Can you tell me what happened?" Charley asked Bonnie in a gentle tone.

"Mr. Foster likes to get an early start to his day," Bonnie said. "I was surprised when I got to the kitchen this morning and he wasn't there setting the first pot of coffee on the stove."

"Wood stove?" Charley asked.

Bonnie nodded. "We haven't upgraded to all the fancy new appliances like the other resorts in the area. Mr. Foster said it was coming once we got things up-and-ru...ru..." She paused for a breath. "Running."

"So, you went looking for him," Charley prompted.

"Yes. I thought, perhaps, he'd overslept. I knocked on his door, but there was no answer."

The alarm clock on the nightstand said three-fifteen. Charley looked around and found a towel lying beside a wash basin. She used it to carefully pick up the clock, which she held next to her ear. "He must have forgotten to wind it last night. Does that happen often?"

"I can't say. This is only our second morning here," Bonnie said.

"So, in reality, there was only one other morning when he was up before you."

"He's always been an early riser," Carl said, a hard edge to his voice.

"Of course, I keep forgetting, you knew Foster from when the resort was operating before the war. What about more recently?"

"I don't remember him coming around much, but then I'm not the one to ask. The only work I've been able to pick up has been either for a timber mill up north or one of the farms in the south."

"What about you?" Charley turned to Bonnie.

"I worked at the local pharmacy and sometimes I'd see him around town. Always knew it was him from that great flowing beard of his. You could have knocked me over with a feather when I got here and saw he'd shaved it off."

"Why are you asking all these questions,

Mrs. Hall?" Carl asked. "I can't see as to how there could have been any funny business going on. Look at the man lying there all peaceful-like. And the door was bolted from the inside."

"You're right, Carl. And I'm not meaning to imply that anything untoward has gone on here. Please forgive me if that's how it sounds." She gave him a sheepish smile. "It's a hazard of my job."

"Is it true?" Hal's voice boomed from the doorway. He marched into the room and over to the bed, deftly avoiding the icy patch.

Unfortunately, Elliot Shaw wasn't as nimble—he skidded on the ice, his arms windmilling as he stumbled backward. Luckily, Freddie was right on his heels and caught him before he fell.

Charley shot a glare at her brother for rousing Hal.

"Hal heard me knocking on Shaw's door," Freddie said. "Their rooms are next to each other."

"I was already awake and dressed," Hal

said in a peevish tone, his arms crossing his chest.

Charley ignored Hal; there were far more important things to deal with than his ruffled feathers. She turned to Elliot, who looked quite dishevelled with sleep-mussed hair and rumpled pyjamas. “You said you were going to check on Foster last night. Did you?”

If he did check on him, she could narrow down the time of death, although why it mattered, she wasn’t quite sure. Something was nagging at her. It was more than the death was “unexplained.” Something didn’t fit.

“I knocked on his door—must have been around eleven? There was no answer, so I assumed he was asleep.”

Or dead.

“It didn’t worry you that he didn’t answer?” she asked.

“I listened through the door as best I could for any wheezing or sounds of distress.” His voice rose in pitch, his face flushed. “I’d have done something if I heard anything like that.” Elliot crossed over to the bed and stared down; a sudden gasp wracked his slim frame, and his hand flew to his mouth.

"Are you all right?" Charley approached him, wondering if he'd noticed something about the body that she missed.

"It's such a loss," he sobbed. "He was a great man. A great teacher." He swallowed heavily and used the sleeve of his pyjamas to wipe his eyes. "I know I was only in Kingston for that one year, but he taught me to love the English classics of literature." He turned to look at Freddie. "Do I need to stay? I need some time—"

"No, I think you've given us what we needed to know. No need for all of us to hang around."

Charley scowled at her brother as she watched Elliot dodge the icy patch in his race out of the room. Elliot seemed overly emotional, all things considered. But she'd learned over the years that people dealt with death in different ways—many of which didn't always make sense. It didn't mean they were hiding anything.

She turned back to the body on the bed

and reached to unbutton Foster's pyjama top. Normally, she'd never dream of disturbing the body before the police arrived, but who knew how long that would be and she needed to see if her intuition was right.

"Hey! What are you doing?" Hal grabbed her hand.

"I'm checking to see if there's anything that will give us a clue as to his cause of death."

"How about natural causes?" Hal snapped at her. "He wasn't a young man. Look at him. He went in his sleep. A blessing we should all hope for. Leave it alone, Charley."

"Easy, Hal," Freddie cautioned.

"Well, she's not a detective, is she? She should stop pretending to be one," Hal countered. He rounded to glare at Charley. "You're a woman, for heaven's sake. It's unseemly for you to be hovering over his body like that."

Freddie stepped between the two of them. "I understand Benny's death has come as a shock. I think we should all take a step back and cool down. There's nothing more for us to do here. Let's all go back upstairs and get dressed. Hal could certainly use a shave." He rubbed his hand along his well-manicured beard. "Not all of us look good with facial hair."

Charley appreciated Freddie's attempt to diffuse the situation, and she had every intention of complying. She turned to give the body one last look and that's when she saw it.

"Look at his face." Charley pointed to Foster.

"What about it?" Hal heaved a sigh and leaned in closer to the body.

"The scraping and scratches along his neck and chin. It's like he tried to shave before he went to bed but made a hash of it."

"So what? We know he wasn't feeling well. Maybe the razor slipped," Hal said.

"But why do it at all if he wasn't well? Don't most men shave in the morning?" It was obvious Hal did. Elliot, too, she remembered from his appearance. She glanced over at Carl. "Do you shave every morning?"

“You get into a habit,” Carl said, rubbing his smooth chin.

“But it’s hardly a hard-and-fast rule,” Freddie added.

“Some chaps don’t want to take the time in the morning,” Hal said. “Frankly, there are times when I wish I’d kept my beard and saved myself the trouble of having to shave every day.”

Charley began to pace the room. “Okay, for argument's sake, let’s say Foster Bennett is the type of man who shaves before going to bed each night.” She nodded toward Bonnie and Carl, who’d remained at the far end of the room. “As you say, he’s an early riser. He likes to be up-and-at-em, ready to face the day.”

She stopped by the bedside, her focus returning to Foster’s body. “Last night he’s not feeling well, so he retires early for the evening. But he doesn’t go directly to bed. He follows his usual routine—a man of habit—so he’ll be prepared for the morning. He shaves—badly. His hand is shaking. Maybe he has a coughing fit while he’s doing it.”

“Of course. See, it all makes perfect sense,” Hal said.

“Except for one thing.” She whirled around and scanned each face in turn—Hal, Freddie, Carl and Bonnie. “Why would this man of habit make the effort to shave but not to wind his alarm clock?”

7

Charley descended the stairwell dressed in her warmest clothes. She paused at the bottom and peered into the corridor behind the reception area. After Freddie had ushered them all out of Foster's bedroom, Carl had propped the door back up, blocking access to any curiosity seekers.

What she wouldn't give to—

"Charley?"

She turned at the gentle touch on her back and gazed up into Hal's face, relieved to see warmth in his brown eyes rather than the cold, stern glare she'd received this morning. His heavy winter coat hung open over a worsted moss-green turtleneck sweater. He was holding a woollen cap and a pair of leather mittens.

"I was waiting for you. I wanted to

apologize for being so short with you earlier. It was such a shock, learning of Benny's death. It was so..." He ran his hand through his hair, his fingers catching on the sandy-blond curls. "...unexpected."

"Those are always the hardest to accept." She had little recollection of her parents' passing—she'd been four years old when they'd drowned. But her grandfather's sudden stroke a decade later had been devastating. He'd been the foundation of their family, the steady builder of the Stormont legacy, the touchstone for their identity as a family. After he was gone, it had taken years for them all—her, Freddie and Gran—to find their balance again. Sometimes Charley wondered if she ever had.

"Still, it was boorish of me and I'm sorry."

"Apology accepted."

He nodded. "You will leave it alone, now, won't you? I know you think shaving before bed is some sinister sign of malfeasance, but if you think about it, that's impossible. The room was locked from the inside."

“Did anyone check the window?” *I should have checked it!*

“Charley, stop this! Please. Let the man rest in peace.”

“All right.” She gave him her sweetest smile and tucked her left hand behind her back, crossing her fingers in the childish take-back gesture that Hal hadn’t yet figured out. “Now, where are you off to?”

“The chaps are taking shifts to help Carl dig out his truck. It’s still snowing like a son-of-a-gun, but he wants to try to get into town as soon as he can.” He took her hand—the one she wasn’t still hiding behind her back. “Will you wait to have lunch with me? Maybe we can go for a walk by the lake this afternoon. There’s something magical about being out in nature and being the first to trample the freshly fallen snow. I’d love to share that with you.”

“I’d like that, too.”

He gently squeezed her hand and left to join the snow-shovelling team.

She gave the corridor another longing look but now wasn’t the time. There were too many curious people around. She'd figure out a way to get back into that room later.

She turned, about to follow her nose to the fresh pot of coffee brewing in the kitchen when an urgent whisper echoing from the landing at the top of the stairwell stopped her cold.

"Shhh! Keep your voice down!" A woman.

"Wait, I need to know. Do you think it's a coincidence that we're both here?" a man asked.

"What else could it be? It was bound to happen to some of us. Don't panic."

"But what if it's not?"

"I don't want to talk about this now. We need to be careful."

"Okay. Shall I use the usual method, then?"

"Fine but be discreet. And keep your distance. I'll go downstairs first. Wait a few minutes and then you can come down."

Charley scampered across the reception area and slipped behind the counter. She picked up the telephone receiver, pretending to be checking for a dial tone when Meredith stepped out of the stairwell.

"Darn, the phones aren't working." Charley replaced the receiver and picked up the pencil and notepad beside it. She turned away and carried them to the other end of the counter, giving herself a few seconds to erase the surprised expression she hadn't been able to hide.

"Some vacation," Meredith said. "I'm going to get some tea and warm up by the fire in the lounge. Will you join me?"

"I'll be there in a minute," Charley said. "I left my watch up in my room and I'm totally lost without it."

The peephole in her door gave her an excellent view of the entrance to the stairwell. Charley lingered in her room for more than ten minutes, but no one passed her door.

Who had Meredith been whispering with?

Suddenly the thought of spending the morning in the lounge with Dan's wife was much more appealing.

But first, she needed that coffee.

She waved a greeting to Freddie who was

sitting with Bob and Sam at one of the tables in the dining room.

"You'll have to serve yourself," he called out to her as she passed by.

Charley glanced around the kitchen, surprised to see Trixie rather than Bonnie stirring a pot on the wood stove.

"Good morning, Charley," she called out. "Grab a plate and help yourself. There are eggs and ham, and I've started a pot of porridge, but it's so late, I don't think it'll be ready until later. Do you think the men will mind having it for lunch? Or maybe a snack—the ones out shovelling aren't bound to be fussy as I imagine they'll be some hungry when they're done." She took a deep breath. "Sorry, my ma always says I'm too much of a flibbertigibbet."

"That's perfectly fine." Charley carried a mug over to the stove and poured herself a cup of coffee. "Where's Bonnie?"

"Oh, the poor dear is absolutely distraught over what happened. I told her I'd take over breakfast for her. Of course, it won't be as good, but..." She shrugged. "We all need to pitch in where we can, don't you think?"

"I do." Charley inhaled the rich aroma and then took a sip. "*Hmmm*, the coffee is delicious."

Trixie's cheeks pinked with pleasure. "It's a little secret touch I like to add. Something Ma taught me. Makes it sing, she always says."

"It certainly does." Charley took another sip as she re-evaluated her previous assessment of the woman. Trixie was young, certainly, but obviously resourceful and not afraid of hard work. "How do you know how to do all this?" She waved her hand around the kitchen.

"I worked in a diner while I was at secretarial school. I did it all—cooking, waitressing, washing the dishes—anything that would pay the bills."

"Do you have a family?"

"My ma. It's been the two of us since my dad died in '42."

That fateful year. "Dieppe?"

She nodded. "You, too?"

"My husband."

They shared a compassionate moment of understanding at their shared loss. Charley was the first to look away; her memories of Theo and their marriage were conflicted.

"Look," Charley said. "I am a terrible cook, but I am more than capable of wielding a dishtowel. So, please, come get me when you're ready to do the cleanup. I'll dry dishes for you."

She topped up her coffee mug and headed to the lounge.

Meredith was seated in one of the armchairs that bookended the fireplace, with Pamela claiming its twin. Charley pushed away her disappointment. While her opinion of Trixie was improving, every encounter she had with Pamela Carmichael was having the opposite effect.

"I hear we missed all the excitement this morning," Pamela said as Charley took a seat on the sofa closest to Meredith.

"Excitement?"

"She means Foster's death," Meredith said with distaste.

"Carl had to break down the door, I hear. What are they going to do with the body? I mean, we're all stranded here for who knows how long?"

Not only a gossip but prone to the dramatic.

"His room is very cold, so it will take longer for decomposition," Charley said. "Hopefully, the storm will be over and we'll be able to leave well before it becomes a problem."

"I'll bet Bob is feeling terrible right now," Pamela said.

"Oh?" Meredith turned to her.

"He and Foster had a *ferocious* argument yesterday."

Meredith nodded absently, obviously as unimpressed with Pamela's penchant for gossip as Charley generally was. "I'm going to the kitchen for another cup of tea. Can I get anyone anything?" she said.

After Meredith had gone, Charley moved to take her seat so she could sit closer to Pamela. "What were they arguing about?" *Sorry, Gran.*

"I don't know exactly. I came down to get a book from Foster's collection to pass the time before dinner." She motioned to the large bookcase behind her. Charley had noted it before. It held all the classics they'd studied in high school as well as many titles she didn't recognize. "I could hear them yelling all the way from the reception area. They stopped as soon as they saw me, but I could tell it was very heated. Both of them were red as poppies—and you could slice the tension in the room with a knife..." She shuddered.

"You didn't hear *any* of what they said?"

"Only what Bob said to Foster as he stormed out." Pamela leaned forward and lowered her voice. "He said 'men like you don't deserve to live'."

The walk by the lake had started pleasantly enough. The large fluffy flakes *were* magical, although having to plough through the knee-deep snow detracted from the overall ambiance. Hal was at his most charming: relaxed and entertaining, reminding Charley of how much she did enjoy his company—when he wasn't trying to one-up Dan.

Without warning, the gentle snowfall turned to pellets of ice. Their hurried return to the lodge became even more treacherous when those ice pellets became rain that instantly froze when they hit the ground.

Carl, Freddie, Dan, and Colin were attempting to shovel a path for Carl's truck. As she and Hal approached, Ralph, Bob, and Sam emerged from the lodge to relieve them.

"I'll give you a hand, too," Hal said, taking Freddie's shovel.

"I can take a shift," Charley said, reaching for Dan's shovel. It was going to take a concerted effort to clear the long laneway. With luck, a municipal snowplough would be by soon to clear the road back to Port Perry.

"Oh, no, Mrs. Hall." Carl snatched the shovel from her hand. "We've got enough fellas here. We only have the four shovels."

"I haven't done any shovelling yet. I can take one of their turns," Charley insisted, trying to retrieve the shovel.

"I'm afraid, I can't allow that ma'am." Carl handed the shovel to Ralph.

"Come on." Freddie took her arm. "I'll let you take my next shift if you're still game."

"There will be no shortage of opportunities," Colin said, looking up at the stormy skies. "If this freezing rain keeps up, we'll be needing picks and axes to dig ourselves out."

Charley glanced back at Carl who was directing the others where to dig. She hated being sidelined because of her gender, but the cold rain had penetrated her winter coat and she was feeling quite chilled. If she was honest with herself, she wasn't all that disappointed Carl had refused her offer.

"Do you have a minute?" Charley asked Dan after they'd shed their winter apparel and hung it on the wooden rack Bonnie had set up in front of the reception's fireplace. It was used to dry wet bathing suits and towels in the summer months when the resort had been a popular destination.

"Sure. What's up?" Dan said as Freddie and Colin headed for the kitchen in search of steaming cups of cocoa.

It was Charley's first opportunity to speak to Dan alone. She had so many things she wanted to ask him, but first: "I wanted to thank you, for last night." At his confused expression, she rushed on. "When they were going on about the war. I could see how it was upsetting Freddie, but of course, I couldn't say anything. It wouldn't have been right. But you did. And...well...thank you."

Dan's eyes danced and he grinned that

million-dollar smile, which still made her knees go weak.

"I have never known you to keep silent when you have something on your mind. Don't tell me you are learning self-restraint."

"It's not that." How could she explain it to him? "The war was hard. On everyone. But Freddie—well, he..."

Dan sobered and his gaze was compassionate. "I know. He feels that he failed to do his part because he was captured."

She nodded. "And those things Hal said to you. I am so sorry, Dan. They were uncalled for. I know you—"

"Stop!" Dan held up his hand. "I don't need you defending me. I don't want you to."

"But it's not fair."

"Look, Charley, we all did what we thought was right, what we thought was best for our loved ones and our country. Not everyone will agree with the path I chose. I can live with that." He took her hands and his eyes bore into hers. "Promise me, you won't jump to my defence again. Not about this."

"But—"

"Promise! And yes, I'm holding onto your hands so you can't sneakily cross your fingers behind your back."

He knew her too well. "I promise."

"Thank you." He released her hands and took a step back. "Now, do you want to tell me about the body in the bedroom?"

Body in the bedroom?

"You sound like Gran," Charley said. "Did you know Mark has subverted her Suffragette Sisters book club so now all they read is mystery novels?"

"Ah, that explains it. He's given a few Agatha Christie novels to Meredith, too. She's crazy about them."

"And you?"

He shrugged. "I may have perused one or two."

"You're pretty *blasé* about Foster's death. You know, I'm surprised you even came here given what you said happened to Elliot Shaw."

"Elliot *is* the reason I came. I never said anything at the time. I mean, I was in grade 9, what could I do?" He turned toward the fire so she couldn't see his face. "I admit that I came here to confront Foster about what happened that weekend. I wanted him to understand the consequences of his action, or should I say his inaction."

"Did you?"

"No. Elliot arrived and..." He turned back to her. "He seems okay, doesn't he?"

The desperation in Dan's voice pierced her soul. He'd lived with this guilt for years, hidden it from everyone—even her. Helpless as a boy, he'd done his best to fight injustice when he saw it as a man. It was what compelled him to stand up to his university coach after the hazing of a rookie rower. It was probably why he was drawn to politics.

He was staring at her with those whiskey-coloured eyes as if she could offer him absolution. They both knew she couldn't, but perhaps she could ease his mind a bit. "No ill effects as far as I can tell," she said.

Dan's shoulders relaxed and he seemed to shake off his melancholy. "Anyway, to answer your question: I don't know how I feel about Foster's death. I didn't like him, but it's possible, in the intervening years, that I've exaggerated the impact of that weekend. I heard Carl and Freddie talking when we were outside, so I know you have your own opinion about what happened to him."

Charley gave Dan a quick summary of finding Foster's body, as well as her frustration that no one took her speculation seriously.

"Not every death is a front-page story, you know. People do die unexpectedly of natural causes," Dan said.

"I know that!" she snapped. "And they're probably right that there's nothing sinister going on. I'd like to be certain, that's all."

"And viewing the body again will do that?"

"Yes."

"You're sure?"

"You sound like you're going to help me."

"You would think, after all these years, that I'd know better." His heavy sigh of resignation was softened by that devastating grin. "Yes, I will help you. But only because I know you, Charley, and none of us will have any peace until your curiosity is satisfied."

"So, you're not doing this for me at all. It's for everyone else."

"For the greater good, yes. I want to make all our lives easier since we're going to be stuck here for a while yet."

"Do you really think it will be long?"

"I'm a city alderman. I know how these things work. Ploughing a little-used rural road is not going to be a high priority after this doozie of a storm."

"And the electricity and telephone?"

"Same. And don't forget, this is a summer resort. It's likely no one is thinking that it's occupied."

Batting away the creeping doom of despair—after all they'd been through the past decade, being storm-stayed in a resort was hardly a hardship—Charley led Dan through the corridor behind the reception area. It took the two of them to lift the wooden door and place it along an inside wall.

Charley went first to the window. It was locked and the undisturbed layer of dust along the sill indicated it hadn't been opened recently.

"If there is no way for anyone to get in or out, how could he have been murdered?" Dan asked.

"First, I'll figure out if it was murder. And then, I'll figure out how it was done." Charley crossed over to the bed and lowered the afghan. She'd expected Dan to join her, but he was rifling through a pile of books on a side table. *So much for preserving the crime scene*. "What are you doing?"

Dan pointed at the bookshelf. "He has KCI yearbooks going back over thirty years. Here's our grade 9 one." He held up a book and then sorted through more on the table. "Nineteen-twenty, twenty-five, thirty. It looks like he pulled every fifth year, going back to when he started teaching. Nineteen-thirty-five. But look here." Dan waved a book at her. "Nineteen-thirty-four. It's the only odd one out." Dan flipped it open and a sheet of paper fluttered to the floor.

"What's that?" Charley stepped toward him as he picked it up.

"It's a list of all of us who are here this weekend and how the rooms are to be assigned," Dan said.

Charley scanned the page. A check mark appeared beside each room assignment, with two exceptions. "How come neither Colin nor I have check marks?"

"The two of you are really party crashers, aren't you?" Dan winked at her. He put the list on the table and started turning the pages of the yearbook. "Here's a photo of you and Poppy, from the year you were on the cheerleading squad!"

"That was a disaster," Charley muttered. She'd joined the squad because Dan had done the unthinkable—made the football team in his freshman year. She thought Poppy was helping her, but her erstwhile best friend had actually been helping herself—to Dan's affections. She returned to the bedside, having no desire to travel down that particular memory lane.

Charley unbuttoned Foster's pyjama top and methodically scanned his body, working her way down from his head to his shoulders, his chest, stopping at his waist. Then she inspected the soles of his feet and lifted the legs of his pyjama pants as far as they would go. “Here, help me lift his arm.”

“What exactly are you looking for?” Dan asked, gently raising Foster’s elbow.

“I’m not sure, but I’ll know if or when I—”

What’s that?

A bump, ugly and raised, and at its centre, a large red dot. She poked it gently.

“Bedbugs, maybe.” Dan leaned closer.

“What about under his other arm?”

Nothing.

“Let’s roll him over.” She scanned his back as thoroughly as she’d done his front, but there were no more bumps or contusions. She buttoned his top and replaced the afghan.

“Satisfied now?” Dan asked.

Charley walked to the dresser and peered down at the open shaving kit. Beside it, a layer of ice had formed over the clear, inch-deep water in the wash basin and a frozen cloth hung over its rim. She stared up at her reflection in the mirror. If Foster had so mangled his shaving, why was there no evidence of blood around?

And now she had another mystery.

"Do you see any syringes?" She opened each drawer and rummaged through them, finding nothing but clothing. "Darn it." She exhaled a long breath of frustration.

"I think we should go," Dan said. "There's nothing to find here."

She whirled to him. "How can you say that? That mark under his arm—"

"A bug bite, nothing more."

"Have you ever known anyone to have *one* bedbug bite? What about the shaving nicks? The alarm clock that wasn't wound?"

"The room locked from the inside," Dan countered. "Charley, what you're suggesting makes no sense. Besides, if that were true, that means—"

"That means we're trapped with a murderer."

Charley and Dan slid the door back across the room's entrance. It frustrated her that he didn't believe her, either. She wanted to investigate the body further, but that would have been too intrusive. Regardless of what Dan thought, that mark under Foster's arm was not from a bug. She was certain of that.

"Hey kids, whatcha doin'?"

Charley's heart stopped and she whirled around to face her brother, the crimson flush of guilt warming her cheeks.

"Jeepers, Freddie, don't sneak up on a fella like that," Dan said, looking equally flustered at being caught doing something he shouldn't.

"Sorry." Freddie chuckled. "I would have thought by now you'd have known better than to allow my sister to drag you into her schemes. But I guess you can't teach an old dog new tricks, can you?"

Dan ran his hand through his hair and grinned back sheepishly. "It seems not."

"Did you find anything?" Freddie asked.

"No," Dan said at the same time as Charley replied, "Yes."

She scowled at her friend and then turned to her brother. "If a poison was injected into a person, how long would it take to work?"

"He's not a doctor," Dan said.

Charley waved his comment away; Dan didn't know about Freddie helping Laine. "It would be pretty fast, right?"

"Well, certainly faster than if it was ingested." He leaned against the wall and rubbed his beard. "Do you think that's what happened?"

"There's a red mark under Foster's left arm that looks like it could be from a needle—"

"Except we didn't find any needles," Dan interjected. "And I hate to keep harping on this, but—"

"I know. The room was locked from the

inside." Charley shifted her focus to Freddie. "Dan thinks it's a bug bite."

"And you don't." Freddie pushed off the wall. "I'm afraid I'm on Dan's side with this one. What you're suggesting doesn't seem possible." He turned a sympathetic smile toward Dan. "Good luck with her. I'd like to believe she's going to let this go, but we both know her too well."

"Well, she's on her own," Dan said.

"'*She*' is standing right here." Charley glared at the two men. "And if I have to do this on my own, I will."

"Please try not to ruffle too many tail feathers, will ya?" Freddie said. "We're stuck here for a while and it would be nice if we weren't all made to feel like murder suspects."

"I should go see what Meredith is up to," Dan said, squeezing past them as he headed back along the corridor toward the stairs up to his room.

"And I am off to meet the lads for cards in the lounge. Do you want to join us?" Freddie asked. "But you'll have to promise: no interrogations."

"I'm not going to interrogate anyone." She was a reporter. She didn't interrogate. She interviewed.

"Oh, there you are Charley," Trixie called from the end of the corridor. "I was wondering if you were still willing to help me clean up the dishes. Bonnie says she's feeling up to doing dinner and I want to make sure the kitchen is all spic-and-span before she returns."

"Of course." Charley brushed past her brother to follow Trixie. As they crossed the reception area Meredith was coming out of the lounge.

"I wouldn't recommend going in there," she said. "It looks like the men are taking it over for poker. They haven't started and already they're getting quite rambunctious."

"Yeah, Freddie told me. We're headed to the kitchen, anyway," Charley said. "Is that an Agatha Christie?" She tilted her head to read the silver lettering on the navy blue cover of a book Meredith was carrying. She only had time to read the word *Tottel's* before Meredith tucked it under her arm. "Dan said Mark gave you some of her novels. He's already turned Gran into a fan."

"No, this is a volume of poetry I found in the library," Meredith said dismissively. "By the way, have you seen Dan? I thought he was going to meet me after he finished his shift shovelling outside, but that was over an hour ago."

"I just passed him. He was heading up to your room."

Charley felt a pang of guilt as she watched Meredith walk away. She didn't know why she'd lied. It wasn't as if she and Dan had done anything wrong—at least nothing that should cause Meredith to be jealous.

Besides, Meredith had her own secrets, didn't she?

In the kitchen, Trixie filled a large pot with water and placed it on the wood stove to heat up. Charley scraped and stacked the dishes on the counter. Once the sink was filled with warm, soapy water, they quickly settled into a rhythm with Trixie washing and Charley drying.

Although she'd grown up in a household

with domestic staff, Gran had insisted Charley and Freddie wash and put away their dishes on the cook's day off. She said it would be unfair to expect the woman to have to do twice the amount of work simply to have a day to herself. Charley had thought it odd that Gran's edict didn't extend to the preparation of their food, but she was wise enough to keep that observation to herself.

Charley peppered Trixie with questions about her childhood and her family. It wasn't difficult to get the young woman to talk—flibbertigibbet was a good description of her. But unlike some who simply liked the sound of their own voices, Trixie had a knack for storytelling and Charley was both entertained and intrigued.

Slowly, Charley brought the conversation around to Trixie's current job and her relationship with Sam Winn.

"We met through the automobile assembly plant, where we both work. A few of the girls from the steno pool went to cheer our boys playing baseball. There's quite the rivalry between some of the factories in Oshawa.

Sam pitched a perfect no-hitter. It was very exciting. After we won, we all lined up for a kiss from the star player. And...well..." Trixie's cheeks glowed red.

"That must have been some kiss." Charley carried a pile of dry dishes over to the shelf where they were stored so Trixie couldn't see the shock on her face.

"Oh, no! It was a peck on the cheek, that's it. All in good fun."

"But something must have happened between the two of you." Charley picked up her towel and a handful of silverware.

"I'll say." She giggled. "After the game, we all went for a beer and he and I hit it off."

"Are you even old enough to drink?" Charley tried to couch the words as a joke so Trixie wouldn't be offended, but she was curious.

"I'm twenty-one," Trixie said, squaring her shoulders and straightening her spine to look taller. "I have a young face, my ma always says."

"Yes, you do." Charley gave her a warm smile. She didn't know how Trixie would take her next question, but she had to ask it. “Does it bother you that Sam is married?”

“I’m not some dolly looking for a sugar daddy, if that’s what you’re thinking. Me and Sam, we’re in love. It’s the real deal.”

“I wasn’t suggesting it wasn’t. But, surely, him having a wife must complicate things.”

“‘We have to be patient,’ he says. He wants to wait until his boys are older, and then he will leave her and we will be together forever. He’s a good father.”

Just not a good husband. Or boyfriend.

Charley ached for Trixie, but she knew that no amount of logic from her would convince the young woman she was destined for heartbreak.

“At least you can spend some time together now,” Charley offered.

The uncharacteristic silence that followed her statement surprised Charley. She put down her towel and turned. Trixie was furiously scrubbing the porridge pot, her brows furrowed and her mouth set in a firm line as if it was taking all her concentration to not respond.

"Trixie?"

She turned toward Charley but kept her gaze down. "It's not quite how I expected."

Charley took her hand. "Leave that to soak. Let's sit for a bit." She led her to the small table with two chairs in the corner of the room. "Do you want me to make some tea? Or cocoa?"

Trixie shook her head.

Charley waited. She could be patient when the situation warranted. Besides, Trixie was a talker. She doubted the young woman would be able to stay silent very long.

And she was right.

"I thought this was going to be a romantic getaway," Trixie said, hurt threading her voice.

"Sam didn't tell you it was a class reunion?"

"Yeah, he did. But he said he didn't have many friends from high school that he was still in contact with, so we'd be able to spend most of our time alone." When she looked up a single tear hung from her false eyelashes. She blinked it away. "I didn't know it would be like this."

“The storm or Foster Bennett’s death?”

“Neither of those. It’s the way he flaunted me to Mr. Bennett.”

“What do you mean by ‘flaunted’?”

“Sam made a point of making sure Mr. Bennett knew how well he was doing—both at the auto plant and with the fact he had both a wife and a mistress; implying—no not implying—stating directly that Mr. Bennett’s party wasn’t important enough for him to bring his wife, so he bro-brought m-m-me instead.” She gulped the last word.

“Oh, my dear.” Charley laid her hand over Trixie’s. “Perhaps you misunderstood.” Although she said the words, Charley was quite certain Trixie hadn’t misunderstood Sam at all.

“No, it’s all right. I’m being silly.” Trixie leaned back and gave Charley a brave smile. “I know Sam loves me. He only said those things to get a rise out of Mr. Bennett. Sam hates—hated—him. He said Mr. Bennett tried to ruin his life. He told me right up front that we were coming here to rub it in the old man’s face—how he’d failed—and to take advantage of as much free food and drink as we could on Mr. Bennett's dime. I feel so awful about it now."

Charley leaned back in her chair, speechless. Did any of the men who'd been invited actually like Foster Bennett? Bob, Dan, and now Sam all seemed to harbour a dislike for their former Outdoor Club leader. What about the others? Neither Hal nor Freddie had said anything disparaging about the man. Elliot, the person who should be holding a grudge, according to Dan, apparently didn't. And what about Ralph? She knew very little about him.

"It's not very nice, I admit," Trixie said. "I've never known Sam to take a dislike to anyone like he has—had—for Mr. Bennett."

"I hate to ask, but were you two together all of last night?" Charley asked.

Trixie's cheeks turned pink, but her eyes held a look of defiance. "Of course. Why are you asking?"

"He couldn't have slipped out after you fell asleep?"

"And done what?"

Charley decided to be up front with the woman. “I have some questions about Foster’s death.”

“Yeah, I heard some of the men talking, saying you didn’t think it was natural.”

“Not being satisfied with the simple answer is a hazard of my job, I’m afraid. I didn’t mean for my question to offend.”

Trixie’s mouth pursed and she tilted her head, regarding Charley through eyes that seemed much wiser than her age would suggest. “That makes sense, I guess,” she said finally. “To answer your question, I’m a very light sleeper and I would have noticed if Sam had left.” She stood up and smoothed her apron. “That’s enough about me and Sam, okay? Let’s get back to work. Those dishes aren’t going to wash themselves.”

What was it Foster had done that had almost ruined Sam’s life? Charley wanted to press but she knew the young woman was done sharing confidences with her—for now at least.

She took the kettle from the wood stove and carried it to the kitchen sink, slowly pouring the steaming water until Trixie indicated the dishwater was warm enough for them to continue.

As Trixie scrubbed a pot, Charley contemplated her next move. She *was* going to get to the bottom of this. Perhaps somewhere in Sam's animosity, Bob's threat and Elliot's forgiveness lay the motive for Foster Bennett's murder.

“Hearts are trump. Charley, please pay attention,” Hal said.

Charley looked down at the cards in her hand. Hal had led a six of clubs, knowing she was void in the suit so she would play one of her hearts to take the trick and control of the game. After all, she was the one who’d set the contract and made hearts trump. “Sorry, I guess I’m a little distracted.”

“That’s okay. It’s a friendly game of Bridge. You can take it back.” Ralph winked at her.

Charley gave him a smile of gratitude and reached to replace the card, but Hal stilled her hand. “Leave it. It’s been played.”

Although they lost the trick, she and Hal managed to fulfil the contract, but only because both Pamela and Ralph seemed to be having difficulty focusing on their cards, too.

Dinner had been a quiet candle-lit affair and afterwards, most of the guests had retired to their rooms. Charley didn't know if the sombre mood was due to Foster's untimely death or from the men's sheer exhaustion from shovelling all day. They'd managed to chip out a path to the main road, but it was another fifteen miles to Port Perry and in addition to all the snow and ice, a number of trees had come down and needed to be cleared away, too. Although disheartened, they all promised to resume their efforts the next morning.

While Hal shuffled the cards and prepared to deal the next hand, Charley glanced back toward the fireplace where Freddie was playing cribbage with Colin, their faces distorted by the flickering light of the candle between them.

"Don't worry about it," Pamela said, squeezing Charley's hand. "I think we're all a little off today. It certainly hasn't been the holiday we were expecting, has it?"

"I thought there might have been more talk about Foster at dinner," Charley said. "Maybe some words to mark his passage. But I guess…" She caught an irritated glance from Hal and shrugged, leaving the sentence hanging.

"You guess what?" Ralph said, his flat tone indicating the question was more of an automatic response rather than any real interest in her answer. His attention was focused on Hal's hands, which were deftly depositing cards around the table.

"Well, it seems that most people here didn't seem to like him very much."

Hal's hands froze and as he raised his gaze to her, there was mixture of surprise and annoyance in his eyes. "What are you talking about? Who didn't like him?" he snapped.

Freddie and Colin had stopped their game to look in their direction, too. She glanced at Pamela, but her eyes were fixed on the cards lying face down in front of her.

"You're not referring to Shaw and that business Cannon was going on about the other night, are you?" Hal asked. "I think it's pretty obvious he was offside given that the supposed injured party is here and shows no sign of distress."

"It's not only Elliot Shaw. I heard that Sam only came here to take advantage of Foster's hospitality, that he has no liking for the man at all. And Bob was overheard threatening Foster." She could have added Dan's reason for coming, too, but decided that would only throw oil on the fire when it came to the tension between Hal and Dan.

"Sounds like nothing but gossip to me. Who have you been talking to?" Hal asked.

Charley noted a very subtle shake of Pamela's head. Okay, so she wouldn't reveal her sources. "It doesn't matter."

"Well, truth be told, I wasn't a huge fan of Old Benny myself," Ralph said unexpectedly. "Given what happened to Gavin and all."

"What about him?" Hal asked. "He was Benny's favourite."

"Precisely. And Benny pushed him at each and every camp, taunting him about how he had a record to uphold."

"Like he did with Hal and Dan yesterday? Egging them on?" Charley asked.

"No, it wasn't quite like that," Ralph said slowly as he rubbed his chin thoughtfully. "I have to admit, I did find that strange, didn't you, Hal?"

Hal shrugged. "Charley, please leave this alone," he said.

"No, she's got a point," Ralph said. "Yesterday Benny seemed to enjoy pitting the two of you against each other, but it felt more like he was taunting you, hoping to rattle one of you so you'd fail. Whereas with Gavin, he was pushing him to do everything he could to be the best."

"And that's a bad thing?" Hal frowned.

"You remember what his father was like. How desperate Gavin was to win his approval." Ralph turned to Charley. "His father was a scholar, but Gavin was a poor student and that rankled his old man. But he excelled at everything physical and loved Outdoor Club. I think he saw Benny as a surrogate father, someone he could impress and, at first, it seemed that Benny was simply encouraging him. But later..." He turned back to

Hal. "Well, sometimes I wonder if the risks Gavin took on Juno Beach were because he always felt the need to prove himself; maybe that could be traced back to Benny."

"He was a hero." Hal shook his head, bewildered.

"It cost him his life."

"It was war. It cost a lot of people their lives."

Ralph's fist slammed onto the table, sending several cards fluttering down to the floor. "I was there with him. It was reckless and unnecessary."

Pamela rounded the table to stand behind her husband and rub his shoulders. "I think we should call it a night." Her calm tone belied the murderous glare she shot Charley and Hal.

Ralph nodded and rose slowly. "Sorry for my outburst." He gave them a sheepish smile. "It's been a long day." He wrapped his arm around his wife as they left.

"I thought you were going to let this go," Hal muttered as he collected the cards.

Charley glanced at Freddie, but he and Colin were studiously examining the cribbage board.

"Don't you think it's odd that everyone who was invited came, even though, by all accounts, Foster was universally disliked. And now he's—"

"For heaven's sake, Charley, the man died in his sleep. Leave him be. I don't know why you want to turn this into a crime unless you're so bored you need something to distract yourself. Isn't being trapped in a once-in-a-century ice storm enough excitement for you?"

"That's not fair."

"What's not fair is you pestering everyone here with your wild accusations. Do you honestly believe one of us is a murderer?" Hal stood. "I'm tired. I'm going to bed; I suggest you do the same. Hopefully, in the morning, you'll see things with a clear head." He paused as if waiting for her to take his advice and return to her room as well. When she didn't make a move to get up from her chair, he turned and stomped away, slapping the door jamb on his way out.

Charley yanked on the belt to tighten her coat as she stepped out onto the lodge's front porch. At some point, since dinner, the storm had stopped. The skies were now clear, and a brilliant near-full moon illuminated the glass-like landscape. The deceptive beauty hid the icy trap that was keeping them stranded.

She took a deep breath, allowing the anger and frustration to drain out of her. She felt empty. Defeated.

The night was still. Mostly. The eerie silence was broken occasionally by the more haunting shatter of ice-laden branches crashing to the ground, the shocking sound making her jump out of her skin. And then, in the distance, a howl. No, two. Three?

"Where there are sheep, the wolves are never very far away," Freddie said as he approached her.

"That doesn't sound at all ominous. Are we

the sheep?" She gratefully accepted the mug of steaming cocoa he handed her. "Did you just come up with that?"

"Unfortunately, not. It was Plautus around two hundred years before Christ. But I've often felt an affinity for wolves. Beautiful creatures, and so misunderstood."

Charley had a sudden, vivid memory of finding her brother, completely naked and baying at the moon—the result of a hallucination triggered by an ill-advised attempt to suddenly stop drinking.

She took a quick sip of her cocoa and scalded her tongue. *Darn it!* "I don't remember hearing them the night we arrived. I thought the full moon brought out the creatures of the night."

"Werewolves and vampires, you mean?" Freddie chuckled. "There was an eclipse, remember? I imagine it affects animals as well as humans."

"I suppose so." She shivered as another wolf joined the chorus.

Mistaking her reaction for cold, Freddie began to vigorously rub his hands up and down her arms and then enveloped her in a hug, managing to spill half her mug of cocoa.

"Sorry about that," he said, taking her mug and stepping away. "Shall I get you another?"

"No, but thank you." She glanced down. Already the thick brown liquid was freezing into the fibres of her coat. She turned to gaze out at the lake. She couldn't face going back inside to clean it off.

Freddie placed the mug on top of the railing. "Something bothering you? Besides Benny's death, I mean." When she didn't immediately reply, he pressed. "Is it Hal?"

Of course he'd ask about Hal. He'd witnessed not only their argument just now, but the tension between them this morning when they found Foster's body. She expelled a long, slow breath, watching the condensation dissipate into the darkness. "I feel like I'm auditioning for a part I'm not sure I even want," she said softly. "Mrs. Hal Overstreet."

"That's only because you are. Isn't that what dating is? A chance to figure out if you're compatible with one another."

"It's not our compatibility that I'm worried about."

Freddie placed his hands on her shoulders and gently turned her to face him. "Then what is it?" He tucked a finger under her chin, gently raising her face to look up at him. "What are you afraid of?"

"What if I never get married and have children?"

"Oh, I can't see that happening. If Hal doesn't work out, I'm sure there are—"

"No, you misunderstand. What if *I* am the one who doesn't want to get married. What if *I* don't want to have children?" The astonishment in Freddie's eyes was her answer. She tried to explain: "You—not only you but all men—get to choose how you live your life."

"That's not true at all. I have less control over my future than you do. I'm the Earl of Thorton. Either I marry and have an heir or the title ends with me. Quite a burden, with hundreds of years of history hanging over me to do what's expected."

"But when you do marry, no one expects

you to give up your career, whatever your career will be, to stay home and raise a family. Once your wife has a baby, you get to decide how much attention you want to pay to them. Heck, as long as you provide for them financially, you're under no other obligation."

"I would never..." Freddie seemed unable to finish.

"No, *you* wouldn't," Charley said, tenderly reaching out to touch his arm in reassurance. "What I'm saying is that you *could*. And society wouldn't think any the worse of you for it."

"So, you're telling me you don't want to get married and have children."

"I don't know. What I don't want is to stop doing what I love because society says I have to. If I could still be an ace reporter as well as a wife and mother, I probably would. But I can't do both alone and what man is going to want to take on some of the domestic responsibilities of running a household and raising a child?"

She liked Hal. Maybe they could work through the rough patch they seemed to have hit, but Gran was right: he needed a wife who would dedicate herself to both him and his political career.

And Dan? He'd proposed several times over the years, but she'd avoided giving him an answer, using the improbable excuse that Theo, who was missing in action, could still be alive. Even though Dan understood her and said he'd never want her to change, his expectations from marriage were no different than Hal's. Mark had been right, darn him. She hadn't truly loved Dan—at least, not enough to give up her career for him.

"You're asking for too much. None of us can have everything we want," Freddie said. "I'm worried about what will become of you if you end up all alone."

She lifted her shoulders in a self-deprecating shrug as her lips quirked up in a half-smile. "No man—or woman—is a failure who has friends."

"Who said that? Aristotle?"

"Clarence. The angel in *It's a Wonderful Life*."

His eyes narrowed and he frowned, still not recognizing the reference.

Charley's heart splintered. It was the first movie they'd gone to see together after he'd come home from the war. "That's all right." She stood on her tiptoes and kissed his cheek. "And, please, don't worry about me. I am in a mood, that's all. It's been a long day."

She picked up the empty mug and went back inside, leaving her brother to the crisp night air and his howling wolves.

Hal was right about one thing: Charley did see things clearer in the morning. She'd been trying so hard to prove Gran wrong, she'd deliberately ignored Hal's boorish behaviour. They hadn't spent an awful lot of time together since his return to Kingston a few months ago, but the Hal that had arrived at Bennett's Family Resort wasn't a man she recognized. Was this Hal an anomaly or was he finally showing his true colours?

If, as Freddie said, the whole purpose of dating was to learn about one another, then it was time for her to stop pretending to be someone she wasn't.

And what she was, was a reporter who'd gone down more than her fair share of dark paths in pursuit of the truth. This wasn't her first murder, and those others she'd successfully solved in no small part because she'd relied on her instincts. Right now, those instincts were telling her that Foster Bennett did not die of natural causes, regardless of the locked door. Someone here was responsible for his death, and she was determined to find out who it was.

But first: coffee.

"Oh, I wouldn't go in there if I were you," Trixie said, intercepting Charley outside of the kitchen. "Bonnie's on a right tear."

Charley glanced around the empty dining room. "Where is everyone?"

"Some of the men are already outside shovelling and the rest are probably staying clear of the kitchen this morning. That's what I'm going to do." Trixie continued past her, back out to the reception area.

Charley pushed open the swinging door into the kitchen. It wasn't that she didn't believe Trixie, but she needed her morning dose of caffeine. And she was curious about what had set Bonnie off.

"Back away slowly or you'll be regretting it." Bonnie's voice was a low, angry rumble.

Her back was turned and from the movement of her shoulders, she appeared to be kneading dough.

Charley glanced around the kitchen, but nothing seemed amiss. "What's happened, Bonnie? Maybe I can help."

The woman turned slowly, her face was flushed and her eyes were red and swollen.

"Are you all right?" Charley asked.

"I don't suppose it was you," Bonnie said. "But when I find the lout, there'll be—" She took a deep breath. "Let's just say Mr. Foster won't be the only body being delivered to the morgue when we eventually get out of here."

Charley glanced longingly at the pot of coffee on the stove but waited for the woman to continue.

"Some no-good, son-of-a-gun came into the kitchen last night and cleaned out the pot of oatmeal I had ready for this morning and disappeared with the last of two loaves of bread, a pitcher of the juice I squeezed last night, and a jar of my homemade strawberry preserve."

"That sounds like it could feed a whole army."

"It was meant to be breakfast this morning. Now there's nothing ready to be served and I've got to start again, plus come up with something for lunch."

"That is so odd," Charley said. "It's not as if we're running out of food, is it? Perhaps, some of the men simply got hungry in the night."

"No one's admitted to it. And as for running out of food? It all depends on how long we're stuck here. We only brought enough to feed the twelve of you for a week. And now, someone's taken the entirety of a meal for himself."

Charley took a mug from the cupboard and poured herself a cup of coffee. "Are we going to have to start rationing the food?" Surely, they'd be rescued before it came to that.

Bonnie nodded. "Aye, that's what Carl thinks. And he says he'll be sleeping in the kitchen tonight to make sure no one else gets a funny idea and tries to abscond with more supplies." She turned away and resumed kneading the dough. Then she glanced back over her shoulder. "If you truly want to help, Mrs. Hall, forget about trying to prove someone killed Mr. Foster and figure out who stole our breakfast instead."

"I'll see what I can do," Charley said as she left the kitchen and took her coffee to the lounge.

Freddie was alone in the room. He put the book he was reading down on a side table and motioned for her to take the second armchair by the fire. "I see you braved Bonnie's kitchen this morning."

"I needed a coffee," she said, taking a long sip. It wasn't as good as Trixie's recipe, but it did the job. "I don't suppose you heard anyone creeping around last night."

Freddie shook his head. "No, I went straight to bed after we spoke. Slept like a log. And you? How are you doing this morning? Better?"

"I think so, but then, I haven't seen Hal yet."

"He's outside. Do you know what you're going to say to him?"

"Not really. But I'm not going to stop trying to find out who murdered Foster and why."

"Charley! For heaven's sake..." Freddie shook his head and heaved a sigh. "What do you intend to do?"

"I thought I might arrange a memorial of sorts. You know, encourage everyone to say something about him—pay tribute to him, if you will."

"I don't think that's a good idea."

Charley eyed her brother over her coffee mug. "Why not? He was a mentor to you and the others. Why wouldn't you all want to take the opportunity to mark his passing?"

"Because you're not doing it to mark his passing, are you? You're doing it in the hope that someone will slip up and reveal something they didn't intend to. But it's a lost cause, Charley. Give it up."

"Don't you think it's odd that so many people didn't like him? Even Ralph admitted he held Foster in some part responsible for his friend Gavin's death." She expelled a long breath of frustration. "Heck, Freddie, from what I can tell, only you and Hal haven't admitted to having a motive for secretly hating the man."

"Are you seriously including Hal and me in your list of suspects?"

"Of course not! I'm only saying that I think it's strange. You know Sam and Bob. Do you know what they had against Foster?"

"I know Sam didn't graduate high school with us because he failed English. Frankly, it was his own fault. He thought he'd get a pass on account of being in Outdoor Club. I don't know about Bob. We weren't that close." Freddie slumped back in his chair. "What can I say, Foster Bennett was a complicated man."

"How so?"

"He was a perfectionist. He always pushed his students to do their best. Not everyone responded well to it."

"But you all chose to be in Outdoor Club. No one made you do it. It wasn't like English class where you were assigned the teacher."

"Yes, that's true. And I'm sure everyone had their own motives for joining."

"Including you."

"Uh-huh." Freddie's demeanour had shifted, and she sensed he would rather not have this conversation. But there was something else going on with him.

Regret?

"How did Theo feel about him?" she asked. Freddie joining Outdoor Club would have been Theo's idea, of that Charley was certain. Her brother favoured more cerebral pursuits but allowed his best friend to draw him into corporeal activities.

"Frustrated most of the time, I guess." Freddie cocked his head and gave her a sly grin. "He hated always finishing second to Gavin in Outdoor Club and second to me in English class."

That's it. Charley clued in to the source of Freddie's change in mood. He'd been the top English student of his year. Coming here gave him the opportunity to share the news of his impending publication with someone whose opinion he valued. He must not have had the chance to talk to his old teacher about it. But she did.

"I told Foster that the university was going to include some of your poems in an upcoming anthology," Charley said.

Freddie blinked twice and frowned. "When did you do that?"

"During the competition Thursday afternoon."

"What did he say?"

"He seemed very pleased. Proud, even."

Freddie rubbed his beard, thought for a moment and then shrugged. "I wonder if it was for me or because he could claim it as another feather in his cap. You know, so he could brag that another one of his students 'made good'." He stood and stretched. "I think I should relieve some of the chaps outside." He took two steps and turned back. "Look, I know I'm not going to be able to convince you to stop investigating Benny's death, but can you please drop the idea of a group memorial for him? If you want to pry out secrets, do it more subtly. One-on-one. You might have better luck that way. And we can avoid any nasty flare-ups like last night."

She took a sip of her now-cold coffee and grimaced. What was going on with Freddie? He didn't seem to be bothered about not having had a chance to celebrate his publishing success with Foster before his death, nor did he seem to care about Foster's reaction when Charley had shared the news. So, what was it? What was making her brother so melancholy?

Charley pulled on a pair of heavy leather gloves in preparation for heading outdoors. She'd caught up to and convinced Freddie to let her take his shift "shovelling to civilization," as they'd started calling it.

She was troubled by her brother's mood, as well as Hal's obvious avoidance of her that morning, but most of all by Foster Bennett's unexplained death. She had a lot to sort through and she couldn't do it sitting still.

She needed physical activity, preferably a nice long walk. Unfortunately, the warmer temperatures had softened the thick layer of ice covering the recent snowfall and it would no longer support her weight. Shovelling through the thigh-high mound was preferable to trying to trudge through it—more practical, too.

Fortunately, Carl, who had been up before the sun, had already gone inside for a coffee break. She didn't think any of the other men would mind her helping out. Many hands make light work and all that.

As she reached for the door's handle, it swung open and she found herself nose to chin with Hal. His cheeks were pink and damp, and there were beads of sweat on his forehead.

She took a step back to allow him to enter and then hesitated. It would be rude to brush past him without saying anything—although that was what she felt like doing. "How is it out there? Are we making progress?" she said, instead.

"Slowly." He tugged off his gloves. "Where are you going?"

"I thought I'd lend a hand. I can't sit around doing nothing."

He nodded and began unbuttoning his coat. "Bonnie doesn't need any help in the kitchen?"

It was on the tip of her tongue to offer a harsh retort, but she forced herself to swallow it. Hal was a product of his social class. While she may want him to know her true nature, lashing out about something he wasn't aware of would be petty and pointless. "If she does, Trixie is a far better choice. My domestic skills don't extend much past telling cook what to make for dinner."

Hal's eyes widened and a grin broke the stern expression on his face. "Oh, I don't know. I hear you wield a pretty mean dishtowel." He winked at her conspiratorially. He knew that she, too, was a product of her upbringing and didn't hold it against her.

What did it say about her that she felt a sense of relief at his acceptance?

"Look, Charley, I think we ended things badly last night. It was a long day and I'm sorry I got testy with you. It's..." He shrugged.

On the other hand, she didn't want to be a slave to the social class she was born into, either. She wasn't interested in living the same life as the women who came before her —heck, even many of the women of her own generation. "I can't sit back and do nothing when I think something is wrong," Charley said. “I know you don’t agree with me. No one here does.”

“I think you’re bored. You’re looking for something to occupy your mind. You probably miss the daily bustle of the newsroom. But surely you must know that life can’t always be exciting—racing from one story to the next.”

“I thought you liked my stories,” she said. “And I thought you liked that I worked in a newsroom—that I was different from all those well-bred young ladies who’ve set their cap for you.”

“Of course, I do.” The rosy tinge of his face turned a deeper shade of pink. Since his return, he’d become the most eligible bachelor in Kingston although, so far, he’d shown no interest in anyone other than Charley.

“And yet, you think I invented a murder purely for my amusement? To keep myself occupied?” She pulled open the door. “I don’t want to argue about this anymore, Hal, so right now, I am going to occupy myself with shovelling our way out of here.”

Charley stomped down the steps and

grabbed the shovel that had been left in a snow drift near the end of the driveway.

Dan was standing beside the trunk of an enormous tree that spanned the width of the road and beyond. He raised his arms and brought the axe down in a smooth arc. Colin was a few feet away using a hatchet to cut away the smaller branches.

"If we can separate this part of the trunk from the rest, we should be able to move it more easily," Elliot said as he trotted past her with a rope. He knelt and began wrapping it around the trunk.

A few feet beyond the fallen tree, Bob was rhythmically plunging his shovel into a snowdrift. Charley went to join him.

"No, not like that," Bob chided after her first unsuccessful attempts at scraping up snow. "First, you have to chip away at the top layer of ice." He plunged the blade of his shovel into the drift and began chopping. "It loosens it, see? Then, you can get some snow on your shovel and toss it away."

Charley followed his instruction. It was a little better, but the weight of the snow made it difficult to fling it to the edge of the road.

"You're going to give yourself a bad back if you keep on like that," Bob said.

"I had no idea snow could be so heavy."

He nodded. "It's the melting. You don't have to fill the scoop. Take a smaller amount and you'll be able to toss it farther." He dropped his shovel and came closer. "Bend your knees and lift with your legs. Don't use your back. Grip it here." He moved her hand down closer to the shovel's blade. "And keep it closer to you when you're lifting the snow to reduce the strain on your back." He stepped back and watched as she followed his instructions, successfully tossing a half-full scoop of snow into the trees along the road. "Excellent."

"Thanks." She grinned at him. "How did you become an expert in snow shovelling?"

"The war." He'd resumed his pattern of plunging, chopping, scooping and tossing. "In Europe, it seemed we were always digging something. Trenches. Latrines. Graves." He glanced up at her. "Sometimes they'd order us grunts to dig a hole one day and then fill it back in the next."

"A make-work project?"

"Yeah, kinda like this one."

"You don't think there's any point in this?"

"Nah. The muckety-mucks think it will keep our spirits up, but I suspect they want to keep us busy so we don't get into any trouble."

Charley leaned on her shovel to catch her breath. "Who are the muckety-mucks?"

Bob stopped, too. "Probably shouldn't say; at least not to you since you came with one of them."

"You mean Hal? Surely not Freddie."

"Nah, Freddie's a good bloke. Caught a rough break, didn't he? Can't imagine spending the war locked away in one of Jerry's camps."

"Hal then."

"Well, the Major is used to being in command, isn't he?" Bob resumed shovelling. "I'm not saying he's wrong, mind you. But a few warm days and some sunshine will do a better job of clearing the road than all of us could, even if we kept at it day and night. Everyone knows it, and yet here we are, following orders like the good little soldiers we are."

Charley couldn't detect any malice in Bob's voice, only the resignation of someone who'd come to terms with having to follow the wishes of another, whether or not they agreed with it. She glanced over to Dan, Colin, and Elliot and wondered what they thought about this. She couldn't imagine Dan acquiescing to Hal on anything. Still, they were all diligently working to clear fifteen miles of road with nothing but a few hand tools. It was a Herculean task. And a vainglorious one.

It was hard to reconcile this Bob Barryman with the one Pamela had described threatening Foster Bennett. Could they have been arguing about teaching? They both worked in that profession.

No. It was unlikely that a disagreement about pedagogy would create such a strong response in someone who'd already been broken down by another vocation. Bob wasn't the type to take on an authority figure on behalf of himself. But what about someone else?

Of course.

"I'm disappointed Nancy couldn't come. But with three kids, I guess it's understandable. We were in the same year, you know," Charley said.

"Were you? I don't think she ever mentioned you."

"Well, we weren't close. At least, not in high school. Still, it would have been nice to have another woman from my class here."

Bob paused mid-stroke and then lowered his shovel. "Were you in Bennett's English class, too?"

"I never had him."

"You were lucky, then. Bastard ruined her life."

Charley remained silent, waiting for him to continue.

"I didn't get to know her until after high school," he said. "She was working as a ticket taker at the cinema." He plunged his shovel into a snowdrift, partially unzipped his coat to pull a cigarette pack out of his shirt pocket.

He held it out to her, but she shook her head in refusal. He lit the tip and inhaled deeply. "She had big dreams, you know. She could act. She's a good actress. And she has a voice that could rival Doris Day's. And dance? Yup, she could do that, too."

"What happened?"

Bob's expression hardened with his voice. "Foster Bennett happened. He stole her confidence. Made her feel small and insignificant. He would openly mock her and her dreams in front of the whole class."

A wave of indignation rose in Charley's chest. How dare he! As if high school wasn't difficult enough for teenagers, but for a teacher to deliberately rob a student of her dreams was unconscionable. "How many years did she have him?" Charley asked.

"Only grade 12. He only taught the senior years, remember? She was so afraid he'd assign her to his class the next year, she didn't return for grade 13."

"Couldn't her parents have insisted she be put in Mr. Littlestone's class?"

"Her parents were already horrified by how

much her marks had dropped, she was afraid they wouldn't believe her if she tried to tell them the reason. Don't forget, Foster Bennett is a legend in that school."

The bile of indignation rose in her throat. The more she learned about Foster Bennett the less she understood why any of them had agreed to come here.

"How is she doing now?" Charley asked.

"Oh, she's great. She's a fabulous mother, always singing to the kids and dancing around the house. I've been encouraging her to get involved with a local theatre group, but she's still hesitant."

"She's the reason you came here. You wanted to confront Foster."

Bob dropped his cigarette butt in the snow and stared down at the trail of dying steam that slowly arose. "I know it doesn't make any sense. If she'd followed her dreams, we'd never have married and had a family. And I think she's happy with her life. I really do. But there's a part of her… Wondering 'what if,' you know?" He raised his gaze to Charley's, and she read the defiance in his eyes. "So, yeah, I came here to give that so-and-so what for."

The tone of his voice, threaded with anger and menace, made her shiver. Perhaps the years of frustration about the abuse that Nancy suffered because of Foster had finally found an outlet for its expression—an outlet he believed he could honourably take since it was for his wife. "You threatened him."

Bob stabbed his shovel in the snow. "Says who?"

"You were overheard saying 'men like you don't deserve to live'."

"I know you think someone killed him." His voice was low, his eyes had narrowed to flinty slits. "And even if you're right, there's a huge gulf between words and deeds, Mrs. Hall. As a reporter, you should know that."

Bob grabbed his shovel and swung it around, up and over his shoulder. Charley held her breath as the blade whipped past her face, but she stayed her ground.

"The trouble with your kind is you like to pretend you're one of us but as soon as you get the chance, you have no trouble stomping on whoever is in your way to get what you want. You and your Major Overstreet are no different than Foster Bennett." He strode past her. "I've done my share of your grunt work for today."

Charley's gaze trailed Bob as he drove the shovel into a snowbank before marching up the steps and disappearing into the resort. She glanced over to where Dan, Colin and Elliot were still attempting to remove the fallen tree. She was relieved they didn't seem to have heard Bob's outburst.

She was surprised not only by the vehemence of his reaction but by how quickly his anger had flared up. It was obvious he harboured a deep-seated animosity toward authority figures—teachers, commanding officers, even those he perceived as being of a higher social standing—but would it extend to physical violence?

Just how close had he come to hitting her with that shovel? And she'd only asked a few questions. Bob held Foster responsible for ruining his wife's life. Could his argument with Foster have triggered him to lash out?

Words and deeds.

Charley resumed the pattern of chopping and scooping, slowly and methodically working her way across the road, keeping her body occupied while her mind reviewed their conversation.

Bob had accused her of being no different than Foster, of using her status, in her case her privileged upbringing, to get what she wanted. It always shook her up when she was lumped in with the worst of her class. Mark did that—regularly pointing out her shortcomings when she failed to grasp how an attitude or behaviour could be misinterpreted. In contrast, she thought back to how relieved she'd felt by Hal's simple acceptance that she wasn't proficient in the kitchen. No harsh judgement.

Charley tried her best to see the world through others' eyes, to be sympathetic to those who didn't have the same financial resources or the benefit of an established family name. She knew she wasn't always successful, but she *tried*—surely that had to count for something.

The resort door banged open against the side of the building as the rest of the men, including Bob, bustled through it, and descended the steps to join the trio beside the tree trunk.

"C'mon, chaps, let's give her a good heave-ho," Hal said, immediately taking charge.

Charley dropped her shovel and went to join them, smiling sweetly at Carl's frown. Dan had held up the loose end of the rope that was tied around the tree's trunk. "It'll be like a game of tug-a-war. Us against this tree."

"We only need to move it enough so a vehicle can pass. We don't have to pull it all the way into the bush," Hal said. "On the count of three. Ready? One. Two. Three. Heave!"

The rope jerked taut and Charley clutched it, feeling the strain between her shoulders as she yanked hard. The tree trunk seemed to leap toward them.

"Heave!" Hal repeated.

This time the trunk's movement was more sustained, and it slid slowly across the road to a cacophony of grunts and curses.

While the tree didn't have to be dragged completely into the bush, the team pulling it did. Fortunately, someone had the forethought to clear a path for them, otherwise, their progress would have been slowed by having to wade through hip-deep snow.

At the point when she was convinced her arms had stretched a good ten inches, Hal called a halt. Sam spiralled jubilantly into a snowbank while the other men roared in victory. Charley joined in, the satisfaction of their accomplishment more than making up for the strain in her back and shoulders.

Buoyed by their success, the men redoubled their efforts to clear the road. Freddie, Ralph, Sam, and even Bob snatched up the shovels and trudged farther down the road as Dan, Colin and Elliot began to tackle the next fallen tree. Carl and Hal were huddled together planning the next step in the great "shovelling to civilization" operation.

Charley glanced down at the measly few feet of snow she'd managed to clear and then back up at the roadway that extended as far as she could see. Bob was right. This was nothing but an exercise to keep them busy.

But even Bob, reinvigorated by the success of moving that tree, had rejoined the effort to clear more of the road.

Perhaps that's what Hal, as a former commanding officer, had understood. These men had been in the war and were familiar with the camaraderie of defying the odds and working together for the common good. Their success in moving that tree brought it all back to them: the knowledge that the little battles, fought and won, are important even when there is more fighting to do.

She gave the men one more glance before heading back inside.

"Oh, hello Charley," Trixie called to her as she scurried through the reception room toward the kitchen. "I've taken a fresh pot of tea into the lounge if you'd like a cup."

"Thank you," she replied, but the woman

had already disappeared through the swinging door.

Charley first thought the lounge was empty as she headed toward the teapot on the table. But as she turned over the teacup to place it on the saucer, she heard a gasp, which made her jump. The clanging of the china cup hitting the saucer echoed like an explosion in the quiet room.

Meredith looked as if she'd seen a ghost herself as she climbed unsteadily down from the bookcase's stepladder she'd been balancing on. "Good heavens, Charley, you scared the wits out of me."

"That makes two of us. Sorry. I didn't think anyone was in here." Charley picked up the teacup and examined it for cracks. Satisfied there were none, she filled it from the pot. "Tea?" she asked, offering the cup to Meredith.

"No, thank you."

Charley took a long sip, savouring the tea's soothing warmth after the damp cold and exertion of being outside. She watched the other woman over the top of her cup.

Meredith hadn't moved and she was breathing heavily. But there was something more—something in her demeanour that didn't fit. The Meredith she'd come to know was confident and poised; it took a lot to rattle her—certainly more than being startled by the sound of a clattering teacup while searching for a book.

"What were you doing when I came in?" Charley asked motioning to the book lying on the floor beside the stepladder. Other books were stacked haphazardly on the shelves.

Meredith's eyes darted between the bookcase and Charley. "I was just rearranging them if you must know." Her cheeks turned crimson, and she gave a nervous chuckle. "I know it's bad form since this isn't my home, but I worked in the library when I was in boarding school, and it bothers me when I see books out of order."

"And what order would that be?"

"By subject and author, of course." She bent and picked up the other books. "If you don't mind, I'll finish up." She climbed the ladder and ran her finger along one of the shelves until she found the spot where she wanted to place the book. She did the same with the other unshelved books, backing down the ladder and turning to Charley with a look of triumph when she'd completed her task. "And now, I think I'm going to go up to my room and have a rest."

When she was gone, Charley rose from her chair by the fire and went to examine the bookshelf.

Reorganizing books seemed like another make-work project. But why not? Everyone, it seemed, was looking for something to keep themselves occupied. Trixie had latched onto Bonnie and was merrily helping out in the kitchen. Pamela was... well, she wasn't sure what Pamela was doing, but probably something. And, of course, everyone thought Charley was attempting to solve a make-believe murder. So, why shouldn't Meredith take it upon herself to rearrange Foster's bookshelf if it made her happy?

Except...

Charley scanned the book spines again. All were properly grouped by subject and author into the usual categories of philosophy, geography, history, biography, and of course, English literature. Forming the bulk of the library, this category was further broken down into prose, poetry and drama. All properly grouped save one. She withdrew the navy blue book with the silver lettering: *Tottel's Miscellany: Songes & Sonettes.*

She opened the cover and flipped through the pages. Yes, it was most certainly a book of English poetry—the first printed anthology of English poetry, according to the copyright note. Why, then, would Meredith have filed it in the history section, between the French Revolution and Napoleonic Wars?

She replaced the book where she'd found it and returned to her chair by the fire. Meredith had behaved oddly when she saw her with that book yesterday. And Charley hadn't forgotten the strange conversation she'd overheard in the stairwell either. She was convinced the female voice had been Meredith's; she'd been the one to come down those stairs. Although Charley had been watching her, she hadn't been able to figure out who she was whispering with.

"Carl! Carl, where are you?" Bonnie's distressed voice called out from the reception area.

Charley hurried out to meet her. "He's outside with the other men. Can I help?"

Bonnie's grey eyes bugged out of her pale, freckled face as she cast her gaze anxiously around the room. Her hands fluttered by her side as her breaths came in short, sharp gasps.

"It's okay, Bonnie. I'm here," Charley said taking her arm. "Take a deep breath. It'll be fine."

Charley rubbed Bonnie's back while the woman took several deep breaths and the colour began to return to her face. "Better?"

Bonnie nodded. "Yes. Thank you."

"Do you want to tell me what's going on? Maybe I can help."

"It's the office. Someone's broken in and left it in a real state."

As Charley followed her along the hallway that ran behind the reception area, she couldn't help but try to sneak a peek into Foster's bedroom as they passed, but someone—Carl presumably—had fixed the broken door, sealing the room up tight.

"I was coming in here to get a pad of paper and pencil to work out a meal plan with what supplies we have left," Bonnie said, stopping in front of a partially open door at the end of the corridor. "When I unlocked the door..." She swung the door wide. "Well, look for yourself."

Whoever had been in the office hadn't tried to cover their tracks. Brilliant rays from the late afternoon sun shone through the window, landing on the solid oak desk that dominated the room. Charley stepped around files and loose papers strewn about on the floor. One of the desk drawers had been pulled out and upended, its contents of paper clips and pencils scattered. A second, larger drawer had been placed on top of the desk, where some of its files were sticking up haphazardly.

"This room is always kept locked," Bonnie said. "I'm the only one with a key."

"Presumably Foster had a key, too." The door hadn't seemed damaged, so it was unlikely the perpetrator had forced his way in.

"Of course, but—"

"I just mean that there is another key out there. It's possible that whoever..." Charley didn't finish that thought. She was the only one who believed Foster had been murdered. "Do you have any idea what the person would be after?"

"Money, maybe?"

"Do you keep much cash in here?"

"No, there's none as far as I know. Mr. Foster arranged credit with the grocer in Port Perry so there was no need for keeping petty cash on hand."

From the way the files had been rifled through, Charley doubted money was the motive. It didn't look like anything else in the room had been touched. "Can you tell if anything is missing?"

Bonnie looked around the room and sighed. "No, I have no idea what the Bennetts kept in here. I presume anything of value would be in the safe."

Charley rounded the desk. There was a gaping hole on the right side where a bank of drawers should have been. On the opposite side, the wood door on a hutch hung open, revealing a safe. Charley squatted beside it. Someone had attempted to get into it, and as with the rest of the desk, they hadn't been subtle about it. It looked as if they'd tried to break into it with a hammer and chisel, but ultimately, had been unsuccessful.

Could the would-be thief have ransacked the room looking for the combination? Was it money he—or she—was after? Something was telling Charley that wasn't the case. Whoever it was, was after something more. Maybe something worth killing Foster Bennett for. "What else would have been in the safe?"

Bonnie shrugged. "I wouldn't know."

"You don't have the combination?"

"No, only the Bennetts did."

Charley picked her way through the files on the floor. Most seemed to be invoices dating back to before the war.

"I can't believe the nerve of some people." Bonnie seemed to have regained her composure. "First to steal our food from the kitchen, and now this? What kind of people did Mr. Foster invite here?"

What kind of people, indeed?

Charley was still mulling that over as she climbed the stairs to return to her room.

When Carl had come inside, she and Bonnie had shown him the office and the three agreed to keep the discovery to themselves—at least for now. Charley stopped Bonnie from tidying up the mess, telling her the police—when they eventually arrived—would want to see it as they'd found it.

While she doubted the theft of their food was anything more than gluttony, Charley refused to believe the ransacking of the office was a coincidence. Whoever had done it was looking for something, and she'd bet her last dollar that it was connected to Foster Bennett's murder.

She opened the door to her room and automatically reached for the light switch, remembering there was still no power when it failed to illuminate the room.

The hair on the back of her neck stood up

in warning and she turned just as a dark form emerged from the shadows and snaked an arm around her waist. A heavy hand clamped across her mouth, muffling her scream.

"Shhh!" The menacing hiss penetrated her ear. The assailant shut the door with a quiet click and locked them in.

Charley pretended to relax into the body holding her. She was sorely tempted to chomp down, hard, on the hand. It would serve him right. Instead, she used her heavy boot to stomp onto his foot.

"Ow!" He immediately released her. "Whad'ya do that for?" He limped a few steps from her. "I was only trying to make sure you didn't yell out in surprise."

"Really? So, you weren't trying to scare the living daylights out of me? Because that's the impression I got." Charley crossed her arms over her chest and leaned back against the door, belying the fact that her pounding heart was threatening to leap out of her chest, her adrenalin high. "You're lucky I didn't bite you again."

"It did have a feeling of *déjà vu* about it,

didn't it?" Mark's soft chuckle and brilliant smile, visible even in the dusky room, calmed her more than she wanted to admit.

"What are you doing here?" She also didn't want to admit how relieved she was to see him. "Wait! How *did* you get here? The roads are blocked."

"Now, that's an interesting story. Which question do you want me to answer first?"

She walked to the door that let out onto the wraparound balcony. It was still locked. She opened the door and looked down, but there were no footprints.

"I didn't sneak in through the balcony door if that's what you're checking. I came in through the same door you did."

"Through the lodge?"

"Yes. I waited until I was sure no one was around and then let myself in."

"You picked the lock to my room? Isn't that against the law?"

He shrugged. "I'm not a cop anymore." His tone was light, but she knew he harboured a certain amount of remorse at the loss of his job as a detective with the Toronto police department. “Besides, I do what’s necessary to get the job done.”

And that was precisely the reason he was now a *private* detective.

Charley cast her gaze around the room. Mark had claimed the only chair so that left only her bed for seating. She opted to remain standing. If there was one thing she knew about her past experiences with Mark Spadina it was that she always had to be on her toes. Besides, it felt strange to have a man, who wasn’t her brother, making himself comfortable in her bedroom.

Mark raised an eyebrow, mocking her dilemma.

“Why don’t you start with why you’re here,” she said more peevishly than she’d intended.

“Grace wasn’t able to get hold of you.”

She’d completely forgotten about her call to the *Tribune*’s archivist. Once Elliot Shaw showed up, it didn’t seem to matter anymore. But if she’d sent Mark... “What did she find out?”

He fished into his jacket pocket and pulled out his notebook. “Let’s see.” He flipped through the pages. "Cora and Michael Shaw died in an automobile accident in the summer of 1934. Neither Grace nor Laine was able to find any records of an Elliot Shaw being hospitalized in Kingston during the spring of that year, but Grace did find a death certificate for an Elliot Shaw, in Toronto, dated November 12, 1935. The person in question was fifteen years old."

"Elliot Shaw can't be that uncommon a name, but the age is right."

"The certificate was signed by a Dr. Arthur Woodley," Mark said. "And with a little digging, I was able to discover that he was the brother of Cora Shaw. The cause of death was left off the certificate, so Grace thinks—"

"Grace thinks he killed himself."

"Bingo!"

Charley paced across the room to the door and turned back to Mark. "It must be the same Elliot Shaw. Dan heard a rumour that Elliot was sent to live with relatives in Toronto after his parents' deaths."

She returned to the fireplace and stared

into dying embers. Before she could move to rekindle it, Mark eased her out of the way.

As she watched him restoking the fire, Charley considered what he'd told her. It wasn't surprising Grace and Laine couldn't find records of a Kingston hospitalization if Dan's suspicions were correct. The family wouldn't want an attempted suicide to become public knowledge. She'd heard of other cases where hospitals reported a generic diagnosis to hide a more stigmatizing one. In high school, she recalled a rumour about a classmate, pregnant and unwed, who suffered an early miscarriage and the hospital reported it as appendicitis.

"What are you thinking?" Mark broke into her musings.

"Two things. First, how tragic it is that a young boy was so unhappy that he felt his only option was to take his own life."

"And second?" He blew gently on the nascent flames.

"Second, if Elliot Shaw is dead, who is the man who arrived here claiming to be him?"

Mark whirled around and jumped to his feet. "He's here?"

"Of course. I thought that was why..." No, wait. Elliot hadn't arrived until after she'd spoken to Grace. "Why are you really here? A fourteen-year-old suicide hardly warrants immediate attention."

"I never said I was here because of that."

"You said—"

"I said I was here because Grace couldn't get hold of you."

"She sent you to check up on me?"

"Not exactly." He lowered himself back down onto the chair.

Charley waited while he adjusted the pleat of his trousers.

"Fine." He heaved a sigh and looked up at her. "Since I was in Toronto, Grace asked me to do some checking into the doctor who signed the death certificate, and she happened to mention that she hadn't been able to get in touch with you."

"That's hardly a surprise. There was a huge ice storm. The power and telephone lines are all down."

"They are down here, but not anywhere else. Toronto and Kingston only got a bucketload of rain. It's not until you get to Port Perry that it turns to snow and ice. Of course, I didn't know that at the time."

"So, you came here to rescue me?"

In the flickering light of the fire, she could see his cheeks turn pink. She so rarely saw him flustered she felt a little thrill flutter in her stomach at his touching concern for her.

"Apparently, my apprehension was misplaced." He stood. "I'll leave you to your winter paradise."

"No, wait!" She took his arm. "I am glad you're here. There is something strange going on, and I could use your help."

And there it was. That arrogant, self-satisfied smirk she found so infuriating. "In that case, Tiger, I'm all yours. What do you need?"

"I think there's been a murder, but no one else here agrees with me." Charley gave Mark a rundown of how they'd discovered Foster Bennett dead in his locked bedroom. "I'm pretty sure the cause of death was injected poison. There was a small red bump under his arm. Everyone thinks it was most likely a bug bite."

"Bugs this time of year?"

"Precisely." Charley pointed her finger in emphasis. "And besides, if it was bedbugs or something like that, there would have been more bites on his body."

"What tipped you off to look closer at the body?"

Charley hesitated and then explained how it appeared that Foster had shaved before bed despite not feeling well but seemed to have forgotten to wind his alarm clock. "I know, pretty flimsy proof," she said.

"Not at all. It's brilliant. Some of the toughest cases are cracked on precisely that type of meticulous observation."

"So, you agree, he was most likely murdered." Charley was surprised by the overwhelming relief she felt. Finally, someone agreed with her. And not just anyone. Mark, an ex-cop and experienced homicide detective.

"You've got good instincts. If you think he was murdered, that's good enough for me."

Charley sank onto the bed. “Thank you. Everyone here thinks I’m making it up because we’re trapped, and I’m bored.”

“By everyone do you mean that fancy-pants Overstreet fella you came with?”

Charley grinned. “Is that going to be his nickname? Fancy Pants?” Mark had a nickname for pretty much everyone.

“Maybe.” Mark grinned back. “Really, Tiger, you could do much better, you know.”

She shrugged. She didn’t want to think about Hal right now. She wanted to get to the truth about the murder. “No one liked Foster Bennett. From what I’ve been able to learn, he was a terrible person who treated others very badly, especially his students. But no one seems to have the kind of animosity that would lead to murder.”

“It’s been my experience that sometimes it doesn’t take all that much. But tell me what you know so far.”

“Well, it started when Dan figured out that everyone here had been at an Outdoor Club camp in the spring of ’34. He was the one who told us that the hazing of the tenderfoots

—him and Elliot—had led to Elliot trying to kill himself. And you know how Dan feels about this sort of thing, so he came here to confront Foster about what happened to Elliot. And then Elliot showed up."

"But now we know he isn't Elliot, so what's his story?"

"I have to admit, I did find it odd when he arrived with no seeming ill will toward Bennett or any of the others who'd been responsible for the hazing. Dan figured he'd come to terms with it. But if he's not the real Elliot..."

"Who is he and what is his connection to Foster?" Mark finished. "And I'm assuming that, as usual, you've ruled out my half-brother as a suspect?"

Charley scowled. "I wish the two of you would get along. Dan is no murderer and besides, after Elliot showed up with no apparent malice, Dan would have no motive to kill Foster."

"You have a point. Okay, who else do we have? What about Fancy Pants? And—yes, I like that name."

Would she ever be able to look at Hal

again and not think of that nickname? "From what I can tell, Hal is the only person here who genuinely liked Foster."

"Your brother?"

Ah, Freddie. He'd surprised her with his admission of distaste for Foster's habit of pitting students against each another, and she was sure there was something more he wasn't saying. But murder? Impossible.

"Never mind," Mark said. "I was only playing devil's advocate. We have to check each person off. What about that lovely young woman I saw carrying tea into the library downstairs?"

"Trixie? She came with Sam Winn." Charley didn't want to tell Mark she was his mistress. "I know poison is often a woman's weapon, but I think we can rule out Pamela, Meredith and Trixie. None of them knew Foster before this weekend."

"That doesn't mean they don't have a motive They could have killed him if they believed he'd injured someone they loved."

"True." Only hours ago, Charley had suspected Bob of killing Foster to avenge the treatment of his wife. “But to solve the case, we’d still have to figure out which of the men had an axe to grind.”

“Okay. So, Sam Winn? What’s his story?”

“Foster failed him in grade 13 so he couldn’t graduate with his class. Trixie told me he was here to show up Foster—you know, prove he made something of himself.” Proving Foster wrong seemed to be a theme among most of the guests. “Bob Barryman came to confront Foster about how he’d treated his wife, Nancy, in high school. He blamed him for crushing her dream to be an actress. And Ralph Carmichael believes Foster’s constant pushing of their classmate, Gavin, led the man to take stupid risks to prove himself, which was ultimately responsible for his death during the Normandy landing.”

Mark swore softly under his breath. He turned to stare into the fire, and she wondered what war memories he was reliving. “And Colin Banks?” he asked, turning back to her. “I saw him outside.”

Charley rolled her eyes. “Honestly, doesn’t

the man have any friends of his own? It seems wherever Dan goes, he follows."

"I wish the two of you would get along," Mark said, mimicking her earlier rebuke of him.

Charley hurled a pillow at him, which he easily caught and tossed back to her.

"What about staff? It looked to me like there's two. A man and a woman."

"Bonnie and Carl. A married couple. They worked here before the war and then quit their jobs to come back when Foster announced he was planning to reopening the resort. Now that he's dead, they don't know what they're going to do."

"What does happen to the resort?"

"I'm not sure. Foster had a brother, so maybe..." She shrugged. "There was something strange that did happen earlier today. The office was broken into, and someone tried to get into the safe. Bonnie thinks it was someone looking for money, but—"

"A break-in? And you're only mentioning this now?" Mark heaved a sigh.

“There were some things about it that were nagging at me, but it’s only now that we’re going through everything that I’m starting to figure out what they were.”

“Such as?”

“Such as why Bonnie went into the office to begin with. She said she was getting paper and a pencil, but there’s a pad of paper by the telephone at the reception counter. And then there’s the fact that whoever did ‘break in’ must have had a key because the door wasn’t forced.” She narrowed her gaze. “Or, I suppose, the lock could have been picked.”

Mark threw up his hands in mock alarm. “Don’t look at me. But frankly, lock-picking isn’t that easy a skill to master. And it would be especially difficult to pull off in a busy resort where you could be discovered at any moment.”

“So, that means the would-be thief either had their own key or stole one from Foster’s room.”

“Do you think this Foster was murdered for something in the office?”

“Something in the safe. And I can’t

imagine there'd be enough money in there for anyone to go to all that trouble." She cocked her head and grinned. "I don't suppose your special non-cop skills extend to safecracking, do they?"

"Sorry, no." He leaned back. "Bonnie and Carl would have their own key to the office, wouldn't they? Is it possible one of them was trying to get into the safe?"

"More than possible." Charley slapped her hand against her head. "She was looking for Carl when I heard her. I more or less forced her to take me to the office."

"So, now we have a bunch of suspects and a bunch of motives."

"But no proof."

"We're not done yet," Mark said. "Remember what I said in the past: sometimes it's the method of the murder that points to the killer. You say Foster was killed by lethal injection. Who'd be able to do that? Any doctors here?"

Charley's eyes widened. "A vet. Ralph Carmichael is a large animal vet."

"There's one. Anyone else?"

"Well, Elliot Shaw said he worked as an aidman during the war, and he seems to have some medical knowledge—certainly more than what I'd expect from someone who claimed to do little more than carrying stretchers." She remembered how overcome with emotion he'd become when they discovered Foster's body. "But as Elliot Shaw isn't Elliot Shaw, everything he said about himself is suspect."

"Sure is. This Shaw character could be anyone. Heck, he could be this brother you mentioned."

"I think that's unlikely. Why would Foster go along with it? But I do take your point that we shouldn't assume anything." She felt invigorated and overwhelmed at the same time. The three most important men in her life—the man she was dating, her brother, and her oldest friend—hadn't believed her when she'd tried to tell them Foster's death was murder. They all told her to let it go. And yet Mark, who had just arrived and hadn't even seen the murder scene, trusted her intuition and was willing to help her without question.

What did that mean? "What's our next move?"

"I think you keep digging." He stood.

"What are you going to do?" she asked, getting up from the bed.

"I'm going to stay out of sight and see if I can catch anyone doing something they shouldn't. Except for the staff, you all are up on this floor. I've set up in a room at the far end of the first floor. It's a little chilly without a fire, but I've put up with worse."

"Let me check to see if the coast is clear," Charley said, walking to the door. She cracked it open and saw Hal's door, across the hall, just closing. "You better go the balcony way," she whispered over her shoulder. "There are too many people out and about right now."

"Or I could stay here." The black brows above his dark eyes wiggled mischievously.

"Duck low when you pass the windows," she said, pushing him toward the balcony door. As it opened she heard a howl in the distance and shivered.

"Are you cold?" Mark put his arm around her.

"No, it's the wolves. They were out last night, too."

She could feel Mark's soft mocking laughter as her shoulder rested against his chest. "What's so funny."

"Those aren't wolves. They're huskies. They're how I got here."

She pushed off him. "You came by dog sled?"

"Well, I sure as heck didn't drive. Yeah, Grace found a fellow with a team outside of Port Perry. We arrived yesterday at dusk and set up camp. I wanted to get the lay of the land before coming to find you."

"Why are they still here?"

"I told Chuck to wait until tomorrow morning and, if I don't get back to camp, to go get the cops."

Someone was knocking at her door.

Rather insistently.

She sat up and glanced at the alarm clock. It said six-fifteen. Who on earth would be banging on her door at this hour of the morning?

Mark?

She shook her head groggily. No, he wouldn't bother knocking.

Thump. Thump. Thump.

"Hold your horses. I'm coming!" She slid her feet into her slippers and pulled on her housecoat. The fire had died sometime in the night and a damp chill hung in the air. She could see her breath as she shuffled across the room.

She peered through the peephole at the intruder.

Freddie's blue eyes twinkled with annoying good humour. Since when had he become a morning person?

She released the lock and stepped back.

"Rise and shine, sleepyhead," her brother said, pushing open the door gently with one hand and redeeming himself by holding up a steaming mug of coffee with the other.

She took the mug and returned to her bed, pulling the covers up and sipping on the delicious ambrosia. The hint of cinnamon told her that Trixie was responsible for this brew. Another early riser.

Freddie knelt by the fireplace and began adding small branches to the smouldering embers. As the flames took hold, he built a criss-cross square of larger logs and her annoyance melted with the room's rising temperature.

When he was done, he sat on the end of her bed and tugged thoughtfully at his beard.

"What's going on?" she asked.

"I was going to ask you the same thing. You left right after dinner."

She buried her nose into her mug so he couldn't see her expression. "I was tired."

Freddie heaved a sigh. "I don't think so. The tension between you and Hal couldn't have been any more obvious. He was in pretty foul humour last night, too."

"At least I had the decency not to inflict my mood on others." She immediately regretted the words as soon as they were out of her mouth.

"As bad as that, is it?"

"No, it's not. We had a disagreement, that's all. I'm certain it will all be smoothed over today." She crossed her fingers underneath the blanket in a take back. She wasn't at all confident Hal would apologize to her for suggesting she'd invented the murder out of boredom. And she had no intention of stopping her investigation to pacify him.

Charley hadn't realized how close she'd been to second-guessing herself until Mark's arrival. His immediate acceptance of her assessment that all was not as it seemed was a balm to her flailing confidence.

"That's good, I guess." Freddie sounded hesitant.

"What do you mean 'you guess'? I thought you wanted things to work out between me and Hal?"

Freddie gazed at the fire for several long moments before turning back to her. "I've been thinking a lot about our conversation the other night. I behaved boorishly when you told me you weren't sure you wanted to be married and have a family."

"It's not what one typically hears from an unmarried woman."

"No, and I admit, it came as a bit of a shock to hear it. But then, I should have remembered you're not a typical woman." He winked at her. "Much to Gran's dismay, I might add."

Charley drained her mug and put it on the nightstand. She leaned forward, taking her brother's hand. "It's not only about how things aren't working out with Hal, or even how it all ended with Dan. I think I would be happier living a different kind of life."

"I think Theo knew that, too." Freddie

quirked a smile at Charley's startled expression. "When he originally told me he was going to ask you to marry him before we shipped out to England, I was against it. He could be wild and unpredictable. He was always asking questions and challenging authority. Hated being told what to do; hated doing what was expected of him." He cocked a quizzical eyebrow. "Sound familiar?"

Whenever Charley thought of Theo, it wasn't the man who became her husband in the days before he left for battle she remembered. Instead, it was the boy who'd been her brother's best friend almost from birth; the bold child who encouraged Freddie to escape from his studies so they could go on some hair-brained adventure; the charismatic teenager who teased Charley mercilessly but then allowed her to tag along despite Freddie's protests.

"I didn't know that you objected to our marriage. You seemed in favour when he proposed," she said.

"It was our biggest fight. I knew you weren't in love with each other—at least not in the way you think people should be when they decide to forsake all others for the rest of their lives. But eventually, he persuaded me he cared for you and sincerely believed the two of you could build a good life together. And... well... you know how convincing he could be."

Freddie stood and began pacing the room. Charley dearly wished she could join him. Her mind was racing, and her body pulsed with an energy that needed an outlet.

Her brother had barely spoken of Theo since his return. It had taken two years before he could even tell her that Theo had died in his arms on the beach after they'd come ashore at Dieppe. That admission, only four months ago, had shattered the storyline she'd been promoting—that as long as Theo was alive she was still a wife and not a widow.

She hadn't set out to use Theo's absence to advance her career, but as the months and then years passed, she came to realize that a husband who was Missing in Action gave her a degree of freedom that an unmarried woman—even a widow—didn't have. It also gave her an excuse to avoid making decisions she wasn't ready for, like marrying Dan.

Freddie stopped pacing and gave her a quizzical look. "You haven't said very much. What are you thinking?"

"I'm wondering why you're telling me this now. I married Theo because the two of you convinced me he needed someone to come home to. I did it for you as much as for Theo."

"I know. And, as I said, he convinced me that he would make you a good husband."

"But could I make him a good wife?" Charley swung her legs over the edge of the bed. She wasn't proud of how she'd taken advantage of Theo's absence, but she assuaged her guilt by assuring herself that when he returned, she'd assume the duties of wife and mother that society expected her to perform. But could she have?

"That's why I'm telling you this now. I don't think Theo would have been happy with a traditional life, either." Freddie sat down beside her. "I didn't see it at the time, but I think he recognized the same in you. I think if he had lived—"

"Don't say it!" Charley grasped his hand. "Please." She wasn't prepared to face the possibility that everything she now dreamed of had almost been hers—that she'd lost it even before she'd known she wanted it.

Poor, poor Theo. She'd mourned for him, but his death hadn't devastated her the way the loss of a spouse should have. Charley closed her eyes, fighting back the tears that should have flowed four months ago.

"I'm not trying to upset you," Freddie said, his voice cracking with emotion. "I'm trying to apologize for not understanding the other night."

Charley squeezed his hand, still unable to speak.

"Oh, boy, I'm botching this up." He took a deep breath. "What I'm trying to say, very badly, is that if there was one Theo out there, there's bound to be another. Don't give up on finding him. Theo wouldn't want you to settle for anything, or anyone, less than what you truly want and deserve."

"Thank you." Charley leaned into her brother, taking comfort in his strong arms wrapped tightly around her. “We would have made a good life,” she whispered to herself. The bittersweet knowledge pierced her soul.

“Blimey! Someone’s at the window.” Freddie pushed her away and leapt to his feet. He was across the room in three broad strides. “Don’t tell me we have a Peeping Tom in the group.”

Charley stilled Freddie's hand before he could open the door to the balcony. "It's probably a shadow from birds flying past. Or a voyeuristic raccoon. I came face-to-face with one yesterday morning. Scared the living daylights out of me. Besides, opening the door will undo all your work to heat the room. It's only now becoming tolerable."

Freddie took a step back. "You'd have made a lousy Outdoor Club member."

"Just as well I wasn't allowed to join, then."

Freddie grunted noncommittally. He glanced back at the balcony door, shrugged and picked up Charley's empty coffee mug. "I'll see you downstairs."

"Freddie," she called out as he opened the door. "Thank you for telling me about Theo."

He returned a wistful smile and a nod before gently pulling the door closed behind himself.

"Sheesh, I thought the professor was never going to leave," Mark said, stepping into the room and shutting the balcony door. He rubbed his hands together and stomped his feet several times. His nose and cheeks were a rosy red, an incongruous look on the normally dark, predatory face. "And you're not dressed yet. C'mon, Tiger, the day's a-wasting."

Charley gathered a pair of tweed trousers and a warm turtleneck sweater she'd borrowed from Bonnie, and took them to the bathroom, along with her thick pair of socks and boots. When she emerged, Mark was kneeling by the fire, adding another chunk of wood to Freddie's log cabin design.

"Let me guess, you were in an outdoor club, too," she said, admiring his work.

"No, but I picked up a few tricks when I was in Italy. Don't believe everything you read about the warm Italian sun. The nights there can be pretty chilly."

Charley watched as Mark blew gently to coax the flames. His admission surprised her. He rarely mentioned his time with the 48th Highlanders when she was around. In fact, the last time it had come up, he claimed to have fabricated the tale so he could gain the trust of a suspect they were interviewing. She hadn't believed him.

"So, what's your plan for the day?" Mark rose and turned to her.

"First thing is to have a chat with Elliot—or the man who claims to be Elliot Shaw. Maybe he'll let something slip about why he's really here."

"Good idea but be careful. Even if he's not the murderer, for some reason he's taken on the identity of a dead man. And he's gutsy about it, coming to a reunion of people who knew Shaw back in high school."

"Barely knew him," Charley corrected. "And that was fifteen years ago when we were all kids."

"While you're with Shaw, I'll keep an eye on the comings and goings of the others. Let's meet back here before lunch. And speaking of food, do you think you can nick something from the kitchen for me? I'm starving."

Starving?

She stared at him incredulously, but before she could ask what he'd done with yesterday's haul, he'd slipped out the balcony door.

Honestly, that man must have a hollow leg.

Ever since their breakfast had gone missing yesterday, Bonnie had been a bear, interrogating each guest about the theft and then keeping close tabs on how much food everyone was taking. Charley wouldn't be surprised if Carl really had slept in the kitchen last night. And now Mark wanted her to sneak more food for him?

"Hello, Charley," Trixie called out from beside the stove. "Did you enjoy your coffee this morning? Your brother was here at the crack of dawn asking me to make a cup for you."

"Yes, thank you. I was pretty sure it was

your delicious recipe." She scanned the room. "Where's Bonnie?"

"Lying down with another of her headaches, poor thing. Can I get you a plate of eggs or would you prefer oatmeal?"

"Oatmeal, thanks." She glanced at the counter. "Are those hard-boiled eggs? Can I have one of those, too?"

"Sure, help yourself." Trixie handed her a steaming bowl and then busied herself with buttering a stack of toast.

Charley pocketed two of the eggs and an apple, glad she'd chosen a loose-fitting trouser with deep pockets.

She couldn't believe her luck as she wandered into the dining room, carrying her bowl of porridge and another mug of Trixie's heavenly coffee. Elliot was sitting at a table, the lone occupant of the room. His head was down, and his full attention was on the paper upon which he was writing. Beside him was a book Charley immediately recognized from its blue cover and silver lettering: *Tottel's Miscellany*.

Now, that's odd.

"Charley!"

She jumped when Hal barked her name as he entered the room from the reception area. She reluctantly turned away from Elliot to greet him. "Good morning, Hal."

"You disappeared right after supper last night."

"I went up to bed; I was tired."

"But you didn't tell anyone."

"I didn't know I needed to report my comings and goings."

Hal heaved out a long breath. "It's simply good manners."

"And who was I supposed to tell? Our host is dead, remember?" She knew she was being churlish, but honestly, she wasn't in the mood to be lectured on her manners.

"I covered for you. I told them you'd exhausted yourself shovelling and had decided to retire early."

"You told them what? 'Exhausted' myself...?" Charley could barely get the words out. "How dare you presume..."

"I didn't presume anything. I merely provided a reasonable explanation for your absence. Honestly, Charley, you should be thanking me. You wouldn't want everyone here to think you're rude."

"Well, I'd rather they think me rude than a feeble woman who gets the vapours at the slightest bit of physical labour."

"You're being unreasonable. I can't talk to you when you're like this." Hal brushed past and stalked into the kitchen.

Charley counted slowly to five. No, things were not going to work out with Hal. They needed to get through this week and, once they were home, she'd talk to him about ending things.

She turned to join Elliot, but his table was empty.

Darn it!

Her appetite had vanished, but she forced herself to finish her oatmeal. It wouldn't do to waste food when their supply was uncertain. She sipped her coffee as she wandered across the reception area. She wasn't sure where Elliot had gone but the lounge seemed a good place to start.

"Hello, Charley," Pamela called out to her.

She and Meredith were dressed for the outdoors. "Are you feeling better?"

"Yes, fine, thank you." Her reply felt like stones in her mouth.

"We're going to walk down to the lake. Would you care to join us?"

Charley shook her head. "Not this time. But it looks like a lovely day for it." She continued to the lounge, but it was empty.

Where did Elliot go?

She slumped down into one of the armchairs, her eyes focusing and unfocusing on the room around her until her gaze landed on the bookshelf. She sat up sharply, spilling some of the now tepid coffee onto her lap.

Tottel's Miscellany had been returned to the bookshelf, but not in its proper section of English poetry nor in the erroneous French history section where Meredith had placed it. She walked over to the bookcase. Elliot had deposited it in the geography section, between the *Rand McNally Atlas* and the *Times Atlas of the World*.

What was it about this obscure volume of old English songs and sonnets that made it so popular? And why was it never shelved where it should be?

As Charley withdrew the book, a single sheet of paper fluttered to the floor. Her pulse quickened and her hand trembled as she picked it up.

The paper hadn't been in the book yesterday.

This must be what Elliot was writing in the dining room.

She stared down at the page. Turned it over, and over again, not wanting to believe what her eyes were telling her.

It was blank.

"Hey, Charley!"

Her head whipped around. Dan was standing in the doorway.

"Are you okay? I said, 'good morning' to you three times." He walked toward her and bent down to pick up the book she'd dropped. "What's on that paper that's got you so absorbed?"

"Nothing." She held it out to him. "Absolutely nothing."

"This yours?" He took the paper and handed her the book. He glanced down, turned the paper over and gave it back to her. "Yup, nothing. So, what's got you rattled?"

"It doesn't make any sense," Charley said, mostly to herself. "I saw him writing on it."

"Who?"

"Elliot. This morning at breakfast. He had this book."

"So?"

Her mind was a flurry of thoughts she needed to find some order to. She had the answer—she felt it in her bones. But...

She'd start at the beginning.

"How much do you remember about Elliot?" she asked Dan.

"Just what happened at spring camp. I don't remember him from any of our classes. He was at KCI for only a few months. Why?"

"Because the real Elliot Shaw killed himself when he was fifteen."

Dan blanched and took a step back. "How do you know that?"

"Grace found out. Nothing about if he was hospitalized in the spring of '34, but a record of his parents' deaths and then a death notice for him, from Toronto, in 1935."

"Wait a minute! How have you been in touch with Grace?"

"That's not important right now."

"I think it's very important. Are the telephones working?"

She followed him as he raced out of the room and across the reception area. He lifted the telephone receiver and held it to his ear. His eyes narrowed and he frowned as he returned it to the cradle.

"What matters is that the man who's here claiming to be Elliot Shaw isn't," she whispered.

"Who is he then?"

She shrugged.

"What? Grace didn't tell you that?"

Her eyes darted around the reception area. "Keep your voice down. Let's go upstairs and I'll tell you everything I know."

"Okay, spill it," Dan said as soon as she closed the door to her room.

"I don't know who he is. And I don't know why he's here. All I know is that he isn't Elliot Shaw—at least not the Elliot Shaw from high school."

"Are you going to try to tie this back to Foster Bennett's supposed murder?" Dan asked.

"Well, it's possible if you think about it," she replied. "Remember you mentioned to me that back then, you'd heard that Elliot Shaw tried to kill himself as a result of the taunting at that Outdoor Club camp. Well...what if he ultimately did? And what if someone who knew him—a friend or relative—decided to avenge his death?"

"It seems a little far-fetched to me."

Charley paced the room, her eyes falling to *Tottel's Miscellany*, which she'd tossed on the bed. "I saw him with this at breakfast." She picked up the book and withdrew the sheet of paper. "He had this book open beside him as he was writing something on a piece of paper. And then, a short time later, it was back on the bookshelf with this paper in it."

"Maybe it's simply a bookmark that was already in the book."

"No, I looked through the book yesterday. There was no paper in it."

Dan took the book from her. "Popular book. Is it any good?"

"I don't know. It's a book of English poetry from the sixteenth century. But it keeps getting misfiled on the shelves. Yesterday, I found it with the French history books, and today, Elliot placed it in geography."

"And that's odd?"

"It is when it's the only book out of place."

Dan crossed the room to the fireplace. He took a long match from the brass container hanging from the mantel and placed it in the smouldering embers. Then he returned and lit the candle on her bedside table. "Let me see that paper." After she'd handed it to him, he gently waved it over the flame.

Charley gasped as shapes appeared on the page, eventually forming recognizable letters and numbers. But no matter how she tried to group them, they didn't make any sense.

Dan took the book from her and rifled it until he found the page he needed. "Get a pencil and write this down." His gaze shifted back and forth between the paper and the book, his finger sliding over the volume of poetry as he called out letters and numbers. When he was done, they stared down at what she had written.

p r i v e t r m 1 1 3 m e e t
0 2 1 8 0 4 k o n e t s

"That doesn't make any sense," Charley said.

"Give me a minute." Dan took the pencil and notepad from her. He sat on the bed, his brow furrowed in concentration. "I'm sure I've got this right."

"How did you know to do that?" Charley asked.

"Because he's a spook." Mark's voice made her jump.

She whirled around and glared at him. "I wish you'd stop doing that."

"Spadina," Dan said, rising. "Why am I not surprised." He turned to Charley. "No doubt the vehicle by which you received Grace's intelligence."

She nodded and then turned to Mark. "What do you mean he's a spook? Do you think Dan's a spy?" She turned back to her old friend. "Are you?"

Dan waved her away and returned to examining the paper.

"C'mon, Sport, the jig's up. You might as well admit it to her." When Dan didn't respond, Mark continued. "I always thought it was odd that a man like Cannon, here, would be content to sit out the war so he could help run Daddy's company."

"Cannon Shipbuilding was a key part of the war effort," Charley said in her friend's defence.

"Sure, it was. And it would be the perfect cover if you were interested in gaining intelligence information. Isn't that right, Sport?" Again, Dan remained silent. "I'm thinking you tried to sign up but as soon as they saw who you were, you were re-routed to Camp X."

Dan's head shot up. "How do you know about Camp X?"

"Tell me I'm wrong."

"What is Camp X?" Charley asked.

Dan threw the detective his darkest look. It couldn't match Mark's intensity, but it was enough to convey his displeasure. "Fine. I'll tell you, Charley, but only because I know you'll be relentless until I do. And I can't have you running around asking a lot of awkward questions."

He put the notepad and pencil aside. "Spadina's correct. When I tried to enlist, in 1940, I was recruited for the intelligence service. At first, I was simply keeping the military informed of any information I might come across since my position at the company gave me access to the latest scientific and naval developments. But when the secret Special Training School 103—unofficially known as Camp X—was established at the end of '41, I was sent for more comprehensive training in espionage."

"Why didn't you tell me?"

Dan and Mark exchanged amused glances, which annoyed Charley. If the stepbrothers were going to finally get along, she'd prefer they find something other than laughing at her to bond over.

"It was *secret*, Charley. I signed an oath."

"Yes, but the war is over. What you did was important. Heroic. Other Allied spies have come forward to talk about their experiences. Don't you want people to know about it? It could have helped you win the party's nomination." *And at dinner that first evening.* She cringed at the memory. "Why didn't you say anything when Hal called you a coward?"

Dan's cheeks reddened and he looked down at his hands.

Mark cocked his head to the side. "Because he's not out of it, are you, Sport?"

"Is that true? Are you still working as a spy? Does your family know?" The questions rushed out of Charley.

Dan turned a pained look toward Mark. "This is why I didn't want to get into it."

Mark shrugged and went to stoke the fire.

"You cannot tell another soul, Charley. I mean it. No crossed fingers. No take backs. This is truly a matter of life and death."

She held out her hands, her fingers splayed in front of her. "Promise."

"I *was* out of it. I was proud of the service I'd done for my country, but once the war was over, I thought that was it. Then, last summer, at the Liberal convention in Ottawa, I got a call from one of the instructors at the camp who said he was going to be in Ottawa at the same time. I thought we were going for drinks—you know, to rehash old times."

"But he had another mission for you," Charley said.

"This Gouzenko affair has everyone on edge," Dan said.

Charley knew about Igor Gouzenko. Everyone did. A cipher clerk stationed at the Soviet Union's embassy in Ottawa, Gouzenko defected a few weeks after the end of the war with proof that his country had been spying on its wartime allies—Canada, Britain and the United States. The revelations had resulted in the arrest and conviction of several civilians from those countries found to be spying for the Soviets.

"My 'friend' believed that some of the refugees and immigrants seeking to come to Canada after the war were Soviet sleeper agents."

"Sleeper agents?"

"Spies who don't have an immediate mission but are placed in a target country and can be activated at some future date."

"That sounds diabolical. Was there

someone spe—" Charley staggered back as the realization hit her full force. "Colin Banks."

Dan nodded.

Charley turned to Mark to gauge his reaction, but his expression remained impassive. *Typical cop.* "All those diamonds. His story about helping out with the Resistance."

"I haven't been able to find anything to refute what he said," Dan said.

"That's why he's always around. It's you who keeps asking him to join you and Mere— Wait! What about Meredith? Do you think she's a sleeper agent, too? Is that why you married her?"

"Of course not!" Dan ran his hands through his hair, a clear sign he was agitated. "I married her to protect her."

"I thought you married her to help your political career, but if her brother is a Soviet spy, that would kill any chance you have." Charley didn't understand how he could be so willing to sacrifice everything he wanted for someone who was little more than a stranger.

"Always the hero, eh, Sport?" Mark mocked.

"Keep out of this, Spadina!" Dan snapped. "Look, Charley, marrying Meredith was the easiest way to get close to Colin. I wouldn't have done it if you'd given me any reason to hope that...well, you know...that you'd accept my proposal. I felt sorry for her and worried she'd be sent back to South Africa where she'd have to live with the consequences of her father's fascist sympathies." He retrieved the notebook from the bed and handed it to her. "But now, I think we've got him."

She could feel Mark's breath on her neck as he moved to stand behind her, peering down at what Dan had written:

privet
room 113
meet Ø2 = 2 am
18 = tomorrow
Ø4 = April
konets

"What does it mean?" she asked. "Privet?"

“It’s pronounced pre-VYET, and it means ‘hello’ in Russian. And kah-NYEHTS is ‘end’ as in the end of the message. Elliot, or whoever he is, is arranging to meet with someone and my money’s on Colin,” Dan said.

“Maybe not,” Charley said carefully. “The only other person I saw with this book wasn’t Colin.” She swallowed heavily and stared into Dan’s whiskey-brown eyes, unsure whether or not she wanted it to be true. “It was Meredith.”

Dan staggered backward, her words seeming to gut punch him. “Surely, you’re not suggesting Meredith...” He shook his head, unable to finish.

“Of course not!” Mark gaped at her, too. “I know you’re not crazy about her, but to suggest she’s a Soviet sleeper agent? That’s ludicrous.”

“I would know,” Dan said. He turned to Mark. “She doesn’t like her?” Then he shifted his gaze back to Charley. “I thought you two were getting along. What do you have against her?”

“Besides the obvious?” Mark’s voice dripped with sarcasm.

Charley closed her eyes and inhaled deeply. *Men!* So easily taken in by a pretty pair of dove-grey eyes and a gentle disposition. She steeled herself, knowing it was going to be an uphill battle to convince them of what she knew to be true. "Look, I don't dislike her. It's just that even before all this, Meredith and her brother seemed to be hiding the truth about themselves and besides, my feelings have nothing to do with this"

"All right, give me the scoop," Mark said.

"You're not seriously going to consider this?" Dan asked him.

Mark shrugged. "Why not? She's a reporter who's used to defending her stories. Go on, Tiger, pretend I'm your editor. Lay out the facts for me."

"Thank you." She ignored Dan's huff of frustration as he stalked over to the fireplace and drummed his fingertips on the mantel. Mark took a seat in the armchair, crossed his legs comfortably, and cocked his head in expectation.

She took a deep breath and squared her shoulders. She tried to tell herself this was no different than the dozens of pitches she'd made to her managing editor at the *Trib*, but that wasn't true. This was a matter of national security—possibly real life and death. "All right. Let's start with the book. I saw Meredith carrying it out of the lounge on Friday afternoon. I asked her about it because I thought it might be an Agatha Christie novel." She glanced at Mark. "Dan had told me how you'd turned her into a fan as you've done with Gran."

Mark chuckled with a self-satisfied smugness.

"She said it wasn't and then when I tried to see what it was, she seemed very secretive about it."

"Maybe she didn't like the idea of you snooping," Dan said.

"Maybe." Charley nodded. "But why did she have it to begin with? It's a rather obscure book of old English poetry."

"Perhaps she was getting it for Colin," Dan said.

"I saw her again with it yesterday. She seemed flustered when I walked into the library and saw her standing on a ladder sorting through books."

“That is an odd thing to do in someone else’s home,” Mark said agreeably.

“She said she’d worked in a library at boarding school, and it bothered her to see books out of order.”

“Which explains it,” Dan said. “It’s not exactly proper form to be rearranging someone else’s bookshelf, so it’s no wonder she was flustered when you caught her at it.”

“But if she was a stickler for order, why was this book filed between a book on the French Revolution and one on the Napoleonic Wars?”

“If that’s what you have, it’s pretty flimsy,” Dan said.

“There’s more. On Friday morning I heard a woman, who I’m certain was Meredith, whispering with a man in the stairwell. He sounded very agitated that they were both here, at the resort, at the same time. She said they needed to be careful, and they agreed to keep their distance and only communicate in ‘the usual method’.”

“A woman. A man. But you didn’t see either of them,” Dan said disdainfully.

"I was downstairs in the reception area and Meredith came out of the stairwell immediately after the exchange. Then, I went up to see if I could find out who the man was, but whoever he was, he'd gone back into his room."

Mark didn't look impressed either, but she refused to let her spirits flag.

"I was with Pamela and Meredith when Elliot arrived Thursday morning. Meredith was most certainly shaken when she saw him. At the time, I thought his presence in the doorway merely surprised her, but I think it was more than that. I think she recognized him and was panicked to see him here."

"Okay, now you're fishing." Dan held up his hands in mock surrender. "If, as you claim, they're both sleeper agents, it's very unlikely they'd have ever met in the past. That's not how it's done."

"Unlikely, but not impossible. She recognized him. I'm sure of it. And if it was innocent, why would they pretend to be strangers?" Charley insisted. "And there's one more thing. It was Meredith's idea to settle in

Kingston. Colin wanted to live in Alberta after they immigrated to Canada."

"Who told you that?" Dan asked.

"She did. Shortly after we first met. I think she was trying to ingratiate herself with me. She said she'd seen pictures of the city and lake and asked her brother if they could go there instead of out west as Colin originally planned. Kingston's proximity to Ottawa, the country's capital city, as well as to Canada's major manufacturing operations would be a far better location for a spy than somewhere out in the Rocky Mountains, don't you think?"

"Taken as a whole you've got a lot of circumstantial evidence—" Mark began.

"It would never hold up in court," Dan said definitively.

"Thank you, counsellor, but we don't need to wait for a jury to decide. We can have our verdict tonight." Mark stood. "You need to get that book back onto the bookshelf. I'll go back downstairs and scout out a good location to keep tabs on the comings and goings down in room 113." He paused at the door to the balcony and turned back.

"Oh, here," Charley dug into her pockets and handed him the hard-boiled eggs and apple. "Best I could manage."

Mark sniffed at the eggs and then shrugged. "Not quite the breakfast I've come to expect from you, Tiger, but it will do."

After he'd gone, she turned to her old friend. "I know you don't want this to be true—"

"It isn't!" His expression was pained and he rolled his shoulders as if he was trying to cast off the weight she was asking him to bear.

Oh, well. In for a penny, in for a pound, as Evelyn had said more than once since she'd arrived from England.

"I know you're also not convinced that Foster Bennett was murdered."

"Charley..." There was a note of warning in his tone.

"Hear me out, please. Foster's office was ransacked yesterday, and someone tried to get into the safe. Whoever it was must have had a key because the door wasn't damaged."

"You think whoever killed Foster also stole the key?"

"Yes. And I wonder if something in that safe is what got Foster murdered."

"Allegedly murdered."

"Yes, counsellor. Allegedly," she said, mimicking Mark's earlier response.

"I think I know where this is going."

"Can you do it? Crack the safe? They do it in all those spy movies."

"They do a lot of things in those movies that can't be done in real life."

Charley picked up the sheet of paper she'd found in *Tottel's Miscellany*. The writing had disappeared and it was blank again. She held it up. "I don't know. This is a pretty neat trick."

"Heat-activated ink," Dan said. He turned away from her and stood at the balcony door for several long minutes. Finally, he turned back. "Okay. I *may* be able to open the safe. It depends on what type it is."

"Thank you!"

"I don't know if it will provide the answers you're looking for, Charley. It's possible that whoever tried to break into that office is nothing more than a common thief."

Or a murderous Soviet sleeper agent.

Charley slipped *Tottel's Miscellany* back between the *Rand McNally Atlas* and the *Times Atlas of the World.* "Done."

Dan straddled the doorway between the lounge and the reception area, keeping a lookout. "Great. Let's get out of here."

"I think we should tell Bonnie of our plan to crack the safe," Charley said, preceding him toward the kitchen.

"So, you've cleared her as a suspect in your murder investigation?"

"No. I haven't 'cleared' anyone." She caught Dan's raised eyebrows. "Okay, except for you and Freddie."

"Not Hal?"

She hesitated. The way she felt about Hal right now... no, she wouldn't go there. She may be upset with his behaviour this week, but she didn't really believe he was a murderer. Did she?

Unable to provide an answer, she decided to ignore the question."Bonnie has a key and can let us in. It would be better than breaking in, don't you think?"

"I'm always in favour of keeping to the letter of the law. It's you who makes that difficult," Dan said, thankfully letting go the topic of Hal as a potential suspect.

Dan waited in the back corridor while Charley poked her head into the kitchen and motioned to Bonnie.

"Are you feeling better?" Charley asked when the woman joined her.

"Yes, thank you. A cold compress works wonders."

"You seem to get these headaches often. Have you seen a doctor about them?"

"Pshaw, don't worry about me. I'll be all right. I think it's just the strain of everything that's happened."

Charley decided not to press. It was obvious Bonnie didn't want to talk about her health, and really, it was none of Charley's business. Instead, she explained that Dan had some experience with safes, and they wanted to see if he could open the one in the office, which she hoped would lead to the identification of the would-be thief.

Bonnie eyed Dan suspiciously as they approached. “Experienced safecracker, are you?”

“Blame it on a misspent youth,” he replied with self-deprecating charm. Charley rolled her eyes as she watched Bonnie succumb to his million-dollar smile, as had so many others over the years.

Bonnie fumbled to get the key into the lock but was successful on her third attempt. She swung open the door and ushered them in, closing it behind her. “It doesn’t look like anyone’s been in here since yesterday,” she said to Charley.

“Before we leave, I’ll show you how to use a strand of your hair to know if someone’s opened the door,” Dan said. He put his hands on his hips and surveyed the mess. “Someone was looking for something.”

“I think it might have been the

combination. The safe's over here," Charley said.

Dan knelt down beside the desk. "Oh, yes. Very common, these safes. Not particularly secure, mind you, but they're cheap and reasonably effective at keeping your average burglar at bay."

"Can you crack it?" Charley asked.

"I guess we'll find out." Dan placed his ear against the metal front and slowly turned the dial. "The trick is making sure you've got the combination length correct. Is it three numbers or...aha, it's four." He glanced up. "Okay, here we go. I need complete silence, please."

Charley held her body rigidly still and tried to breathe only when necessary. She watched intently as Dan slowly rotated the dial clockwise, then counter-clockwise. He muttered a curse under his breath, spun the dial fully around several times and started again. He repeated the process at least a dozen times before finally removing his hand from the dial and leaning back on his heels.

"No luck?" Charley tried to hide her disappointment.

Dan stood and pointed to the handle that hung below the combination dial. "I thought you'd like to do the honours."

"Really?" She felt as giddy as a child on Christmas morning as she tentatively took the handle. She looked up at him.

"Lift and pull toward yourself. As long as you don't jostle the dial, it will be fine."

Charley counted to three and then followed Dan's instructions. Miraculously the door swung open, and she expelled a yelp of excitement. "You did it!"

Bonnie knelt beside her and peered inside. "There's not much here, is there?"

Charley took a closer look. She didn't know what she'd been expecting. Mountains of cash, maybe? Something worth stealing. But Bonnie was right. All she could see was a thin, white envelope. She pulled it out and read the name embossed along the top: *Morley & Ross, Solicitors*. The envelope was unsealed and she withdrew a slim document. "In the matter of the execution of a Will of Anderson Bennett," she read.

"Mr. Foster's father," Bonnie said.

Charley ran her hand along the inside of the safe in case she'd missed anything, but no, the only item in the safe was the will.

"Can I see that?" Dan asked and she handed it to him. "I don't generally deal with personal documents, but I did have to take some estate law courses to get my degree." He scanned the first page. "Drawn up in 1936. Everything to his wife, Rosemary."

"Poor Mrs. Bennett, she passed away about three years ago. Dear sweet thing, it was probably caring for him that killed her."

"Why do you say that?" Charley asked.

"Mr. Bennett was one of those men that did as he pleased. Ate too much, drank too much, smoked too much. Eventually, his bad habits caught up with him. Lost his foot in '42 and a year later he went blind. After that, she had to do everything for him."

"How did he manage after she was gone?" Charley asked.

"He went to live with Mr. Fraser, in

Peterborough. In the summer months, they lived here. I'd see Mr. Fraser when he came into town to pick up medication for his dad at the pharmacy where I worked."

"Who's Fraser? Oh wait, never mind, I see it here. Foster's brother." Dan began reading: "'If my said wife shall have predeceased me, I give all my property whatsoever situate to my two sons, Foster and Fraser, to be shared equally and in such a manner that one cannot dispose of without the consent of the other.'" Dan emitted a long whistle.

"What does that mean?" Charley asked.

"Wait a minute." Dan continued reading silently to himself and then handed the will back to Charley. "Basically, the entirety of his estate is this resort. The brothers have to either own it jointly or sell it jointly. And they are forbidden from selling to the other."

Charley stared down at the document. "Is that a bad thing?"

"Unusual to say the least. Bonnie, did the brothers get along?"

"As well as any two brothers, I imagine. I didn't see them together all that often. The last time would have been at their dad's funeral, before Christmas."

"You've heard of a shotgun wedding?" Dan asked Charley. "Well, think of this as a shotgun will. The brothers are forced to act together."

"What happens if one of them dies?" Charley asked.

"Then the surviving brother gets everything—no strings attached."

"And if they're both gone?" Bonnie asked.

Dan shrugged. "The will makes no provision for that, so I assume this resort would be auctioned off by the province."

Bonnie pulled shut the office door and locked it, pocketing the key. "I best start preparing dinner," she said and headed off toward the kitchen.

"Well, I think it's pretty clear that whoever broke into the office was simply looking for easy money," Dan said. "Although I hate to think we have a thief among us."

"How can you say that?" Charley whirled around to face him. "You admitted the will was unusual."

"Sure, but so what? People make unusual bequests all the time. Even if I believed Foster was murdered, how does knowing the contents of the will help us? It certainly doesn't provide a motive for Elliot Shaw to kill him."

"Unless there was some reason the

Soviets wanted to get their hands on this property? Perhaps to set up their own spy school?" Charley suggested.

"In which case, they'd also have to do away with the brother, remember?" Dan sighed. "And there are far easier ways to purchase property in this province without resorting to murder."

"I don't think all of these events are a mere coincidence: Foster dies, his office is broken into, *and* we discover Russian sleeper agents all in the same weekend." She saw Dan hesitate. "Do you?"

"The only thing that I think isn't a coincidence is that Elliot and Colin are here together. I think they used Foster's invitation to arrange a meeting."

"But you invited Colin."

"Yes, and I think he reached out to his contact, the man posing as Elliot, and invited him. Remember, Elliot didn't arrive until the second day—after I told everyone that I believed Elliot had attempted suicide and went to live with relatives after his parents were killed in a car accident."

Charley chewed the inside of her cheek. Dan's speculation had some merit, but was Meredith she saw with the book. It was Meredith she overheard in the stairwell. And it was apparent from that whispered conversation, as well as her reaction to Elliot's arrival, that the meeting between the two was unexpected.

Charley knew she'd never be able to convince Dan that his wife was the second sleeper agent. When she'd suggested it earlier, he was shocked and adamant that it couldn't possibly be true. She decided to drop it for the time being. The truth would be revealed soon enough.

"I think I hear the ladies returning from their walk," Dan said.

Charley followed him back out to the reception area. Meredith and Pamela were hanging their scarves and mittens on the rack in front of the fire.

"You should have come, Charley. It was absolutely glorious," Pamela said.

"With any luck, all this sunshine should melt the ice and clear the road so we can be on our way," Meredith said. "I thought you were going to go out and help with the shovelling," she added, turning her cheek to receive a light kiss from Dan.

"Bonnie needed some help in the kitchen, so Charley and I pitched in."

Charley stumbled, astounded by how quickly the lie came to Dan. But then again, he hadn't told her that he worked for military intelligence, so should she really be surprised at how easily he'd created this small deception? It unnerved her, though. What else had he kept from her? Was keeping from her still? How much did she know about the person she thought she knew best in the world? And if he could so easily fool her, what did that say about all her other relationships?

"As lovely as the day was, I am looking forward to warming up with a nice cup of tea in the lounge," Pamela said.

"I'll join you," Dan said.

"Oh, how nice," Meredith replied. " But are you sure you shouldn't be outside with the others?"

"I'll take my turn later," Dan said, taking

his wife's arm and escorting her into the lounge.

"What about you, Charley? Care to join us?" Pamela asked.

"Um... no, thank you. I should really..." She shrugged apologetically, annoyed that she couldn't fabricate an excuse as quickly as Dan had been able to.

She slowly climbed the stairs to the second floor. She'd intended to join the women, to keep an eye on Meredith, until Dan had stepped in. Maybe he did have some small measure of doubt about his wife, after all.

Or maybe he was trying to protect Meredith from Charley. The thought depressed her, but then everything about this situation depressed her. What did it say about their friendship if Dan was more willing to put his faith in a woman he'd known for less than a year than he was in Charley, his lifelong friend?

"Charley, we need to talk." Hal stepped out of his room just as she approached her room.

Had he been standing at his door, staring through the peephole?

"Can it wait?" She slipped her key into the lock. She didn't want to go another round with him after the morning she'd had.

"No, I don't think it can." He followed her in and shut the door. "There's no easy way to say this, but it's not going to work out between us. I can't be with someone who makes outrageous accusations and embarrasses me in front of my colleagues. And quite frankly, I am surprised by your lack of decorum and proper etiquette considering your family."

Charley took a step back and swayed slightly as his words knifed their way into her.

"I think, once we get home, we should go our separate ways," he said.

"Of course." She forced the words past her clenched jaw. Her fists balled at her sides.

"No hard feelings, right?"

"None, at all."

"All right then." Hal sounded inordinately relieved. "I guess I'll see you at dinner."

He was careful to gently close the door as he left, which further infuriated her.

"Well, I said it before, you're too good for him."

"Shut up, Mark." Charley stomped across the room and tossed a log onto the fire. "What are you doing here, anyway? I thought you were keeping an eye on room 113."

"I wanted to know what happened with Shaw. But hey..." He took her arm, led her to the armchair and knelt beside her. "You are better off without him. You know that right?"

Charley gazed into his dark eyes. They were deep brown, like a rich, dark coffee, not the menacing black glare she was used to. Even his voice was different, smooth silk rather than its usual rough leather. This wasn't the Mark she knew, and she was struck, once again, by how poor a judge of a person's character she must be.

"Of course, I know that! And I know the relationship wasn't going to work out. I was going to tell him so as soon as we got home." She pushed Mark away and stood up. "But Jiminy Cricket, he accuses *me* of lacking proper etiquette and then he goes and breaks things off before the week's even over."

"Wait a minute." Mark came to his feet. "You're upset that he beat you to the punch?"

"No. I'm upset that he didn't wait until we were back in Kingston. Now, we have who knows how many days left where we have to act as if everything is fine between us."

"But if you knew you were breaking up, what difference does it make? You'd be faking anyway, wouldn't you?"

Did he not understand? "Yes, but we'd be able to pretend with each other that we didn't know, which would make things a lot easier—especially on the long car ride home."

Mark cocked his head to the side and seemed to be trying to see her from a different angle. "No, I don't get it. Self-delusion must be an advantage of your class. We poor Joes can't afford to live in dreamland. In any event, you don't have to go back to Kingston with him, Tiger. I'd be happy to drive you."

Three loud raps on the door interrupted

the snarky response that was on the tip of her tongue.

Charley let Dan into the room. "Where's Meredith?" she asked.

"Taking a nap. And before you ask, no she didn't take the book. She didn't even glance in the direction of the bookcase, so I think you're barking up the wrong tree."

Well, at least she'd planted the seed of doubt. Not that it would make it any easier on Dan when it came to fruition.

"Did you tell Spadina about the will?" Dan asked.

"I hadn't got there yet," Charley said and proceeded to update Mark on what they'd learned.

"It's the brother," Mark said when she finished.

"The brother what?" Dan asked. "Are you suggesting that he's hiding somewhere around here and that he tried to break into the safe? Or maybe you think he's pretending to be Elliot." He gave an impatient snort. "I think Bonnie, who knows both the brothers, would have recognized him, don't you think?"

"I'm only pointing out that Fraser Bennett had a motive to kill his brother, Foster," Mark said calmly.

"Jeepers, you're as crazy as she is!" Dan grumbled. "Once and for all, there was no murder. Can we please focus on Elliot and Colin?" He lowered his gaze and took a deep breath. "I'm sorry. Look, we're so close to being able to catch a pair of Soviet spies, I don't want us to get distracted and blow it."

"Forget about it, Sport," Mark patted him on the back, grinning magnanimously now that he had the upper hand. "I did a bit of reconnaissance while you two were gone. Room 113 is the last room down the hall, right next to the exit. We can set up an observation post in 114, across the hall, and a listening post next door in 111."

"When do you think the help from the outside will get here?" Charley asked.

"Not in time," Mark said. "Even if Chuck got back to Port Perry before noon, it would still take a while for him to convince the authorities that we need rescuing, and then for them to coordinate a team. I'd say tomorrow morning would be the earliest we could hope for—and even then, I couldn't guarantee it would be anything more than a lonely snowplough driver."

"So, it's to be the three of us," she said.

"I think we're going to need another man," Mark said. "No offence to you, Charley, but we're going to have to apprehend two individuals, and that would be easier with four of us rather than three."

"I agree," Dan said, "but this is a delicate and dangerous mission with ramifications for national security. Given all the lying and thieving that's been going on, I don't know if there's anyone here we can trust?"

"I know one person," Charley said.

Charley stepped back from the peephole of room 114 to glance down, squinting to read the time on her watch in the darkened room. *Two-twelve a.m.* She stifled a yawn and placed her eye against the peephole to resume her observation of the room across the hall. Although she hadn't seen anyone go in, she knew room 113 wasn't empty.

Mark and Freddie were hiding outside to keep watch on the room's patio entrance. Freddie had snuck back to let her know that Elliot had entered the room that way shortly before two a.m., but as far as she knew, his contact hadn't yet arrived.

Their plan had as many holes as a block of Swiss cheese.

Dan had reluctantly agreed to remain in his room until after the appointed meeting time in case Meredith was the spy. Then, he was to come down and join Charley.

They'd synchronized their watches and would move in at two-forty-five—unless the parties dispersed before then, in which case they'd nab them as they left.

There was no contingency for what to do if one of the pair didn't show up.

But the biggest hole, as far as she was concerned, was going to be their lack of evidence. They'd hoped to be able to listen to the conversation from the adjacent room, but Mark had nixed that idea. He claimed they needed all four of them to cover the exits and besides, he'd checked, and it was virtually impossible to hear anything through the walls of room 111. It sounded fishy to Charley, but she acquiesced—after all, Mark had more experience in these things.

Charley turned as the patio door behind her swooshed open and Dan stepped into the room, bringing with him a rush of cold air. In the darkness, she could only detect his shadow, but she knew it was him from the way he moved.

"Meredith is still asleep," he said before Charley could ask.

She nodded, a little disappointed. But it didn't mean she was wrong. Maybe Meredith never got the message. Another hole they hadn't plugged.

"I don't think the second spy has arrived yet," she said. "Elliot is in there, though. What do you think we should do?"

"Let's give it some time. These things don't always run on schedule."

Charley stepped aside so Dan could replace her at the peephole. "At least we'll get Elliot, though. Right?"

"Hmm. Maybe."

"What do you mean? If he's a Russian spy, we have to catch him."

"Not necessarily. It's Colin I'm after. If we've identified this fake Elliot as his contact, it might be better to sit on him and see what he does. Maybe he'll lead us to others," Dan whispered while continuing to stare through the hole at the door across the hall.

"So, we do nothing? Just let him go?"

Dan glanced back at her. "I know it goes

against the grain, Charley, but that may be our best course of action." He turned back to the door. "Unlike what you see in the movies, intelligence is a game of patience—not your strong suit, I know."

How many times had Mark said the same thing when they were pursuing a suspect? "I'm getting better," she said, although Dan would question that if he could see her pacing behind him.

The patio door opened again, and Mark entered. "The second spy just went in through the patio."

"Who is it? Could you tell?" Charley asked.

Mark shook his head. "Can't say for sure. It was dark and they were dressed in black. Hooded."

"All right." Dan looked at his watch. "It's two-forty. Let's go in five minutes as planned."

Mark nodded, touched his hip, where Charley knew he carried his pistol, and left without another word.

Dan reached around to the small of his back and withdrew a revolver from his belt.

"You have a gun?" Charley said stupidly.

"Of course I have a gun."

"No, I mean, you have a gun *here*. You brought it on vacation, as if you were expecting trouble."

"I always have it with me when Colin's around." Dan swung open the cylinder and loaded six bullets from his pocket into the chamber. "When we go in, just remember, all you need to do is flood the room with light from your flashlight to surprise them. Stay back. You and Freddie are there for support in case they get past us. Let me and Spadina handle the action."

Charley expelled a huff of frustration. "I know, I know. We're backup."

Dan's eyes narrowed as he stared intently into hers. "I'm not kidding, Charley. This is as serious as it gets. I don't want you to get hurt."

She shrugged him off. "I've been in tough situations before," she said, remembering the shootout she and Mark found themselves in several months earlier. And then there was the time Colin's wife had tried to kill her. And that rogue cop. And...

When she thought about it, ever since Mark had come to town, she'd found herself in more than her fair share of tough situations.

"Okay, I'll hang back." Truth was, she wasn't keen to get in the middle of another gun battle anyway.

Dan looked at his watch. "Ready?" he asked, removing the revolver's safety.

Charley rubbed her palms along her thighs and picked up the flashlight from the floor beside the door. Her body buzzed in anticipation. "Ready."

Dan slowly opened the door and held up his hand. Then three fingers. Two fingers. One.

Even though she was ready for it, the explosion of motion caught Charley by surprise. In an instant, Dan was across the hall and had kicked open the door to room 113. She pushed the button to turn on the flashlight as he yelled out, "No one move!"

At the same time, she heard Mark bark out, "Show me your hands!" and a bright beam from Freddie's flashlight shone into the room from the direction of the patio door.

The spies offered no resistance, and it was over quickly. As Charley entered the room, Dan and Mark were each kneeling over a prone suspect.

"Is this a robbery?" Elliot's voice squeaked.

"You'll wish it was," Mark said.

"Mark Spadina?"

Charley's heart broke for Dan. Meredith had asked the question.

Mark turned over the person he'd been restraining. "Sorry, Angel. I was hoping Charley was wrong, but..."

Charley pointed the flashlight toward the woman and immediately wished she hadn't. Meredith's pale eyes glared at her with such loathing Charley took a cautious step back even though she knew Mark had her well secured.

"I should have known you'd be behind this," she spat. "Every time I turn around, there you are. The great, gutsy, glorious Charley Hall. In reality, you're nothing more than a boil I should have lanced from the very start."

Charley glanced at Dan. To his credit, his grip on Elliot hadn't weakened although it was obvious from his stony expression that the confirmation his wife was the second spy had devastated him.

"Now, that's not nice," Mark said, pulling Meredith to her feet. He slipped one end of his handcuffs onto her wrist.

"Handcuffs, detective? Really?" she said with derision.

"Never travel without them." Mark led her over to the bed instructing her to sit and scoot backwards until her back was against the metal headboard.

Dan pulled Elliot to his feet and dragged him toward the bed, too. With Freddie's assistance, he lifted him onto the mattress and plopped him down next to Meredith.

Mark slipped the cuffs through the metal slat of the headboard and snapped the other bracelet around Elliot's wrist.

"There. Nice and cozy," Mark said, stepping back.

"What is all this about?" Elliot asked,

turning his head to avoid the twin beams from Charley's and Freddie's flashlights.

"Don't say anything!" Meredith said. She looked up at Dan and shrugged. "So, you caught us having an affair. So what?"

"You were still in bed when I left." The fact Dan's statement sounded more like a question told Charley he was still having trouble accepting that his wife was a spy.

"And I thought you were, too," Meredith said.

"You didn't check closely enough. I'd arranged the pillows so it would seem I was still beside you."

"I didn't even feel you get up." Meredith's eyes narrowed and her head cocked to the side as she studied her husband. "You're not just a lawyer, are you?" When Dan didn't reply she continued. "Huh. I underestimated you. I thought I was playing you, but it seems you were playing me."

"I thought it was Colin," he said.

"Colin?" Meredith said with disdain. "My brother is so enamoured with your country and its parliamentary system, it makes me sick. Look at you. Look at her!" She pointed to Charley and then turned to Mark. "You know what I mean. Their money. Their entitlement. How can you stand it?"

"I can stand it because I believe people should be rewarded if they work hard and recognized if they contribute to society," Mark said. "Dan and Charley may come from money, but I don't see them sitting at home eating bonbons while they make money off the backs of others. Dan not only works for his family's shipbuilding company but he's dedicated his life to public service. And Charley? She's risked her life more than once to expose corruption in her city. What have you done, Meredith, aside from marry a rich man and wait around to be told what to do by your Soviet bosses?"

Charley gaped in surprise at Mark's response. She glanced at Dan and saw by his raised eyebrows that he was equally astonished. Praise from Mark wasn't something he was used to. She had to wonder if the detective was being sincere or simply trying to get under Meredith's skin. If she were to ask him, of course, he would claim it was the latter. But she suspected there was a grudging feeling of admiration forming between the brothers.

"But enough about that. We're not here to debate politics," Mark said. "I want to know who this fellow is." He pointed to Elliot.

"I'm Elliot Sh—"

"Give it up!" Mark interjected. "We know the real Elliot Shaw killed himself when he was fifteen."

"I'm not saying another word." Elliot leaned back and closed his eyes.

"Just what do you think is going on?" Meredith asked. "Why did you break in here?"

"We deciphered the note Elliot left for you in that book. We know you're both Soviet spies," Dan said.

Meredith elbowed Elliot. "You stupid, stupid man. I told you to ignore us both being here. Now you've ruined everything."

Elliot grunted but kept his eyes closed.

"How do you know each other," Dan asked.

"You might as well tell us," Mark added.

"The authorities will be here in the morning, and it'll all come out then."

"Fine. It doesn't matter anyway," Meredith said, lifting her chin, her eyes cold, haughty. "There are too many of us already here. I couldn't tell you who they are even if you torture me. That's the way the Commissariat works. We aren't supposed to know each other." Her boastful tone made it seem as if she was happy to be caught because now, she could show off her superiority. "It was pure coincidence that I recognized this poltroon from a meeting of the Communist party that we attended in Zurich during the war."

"While you were in boarding school?" Charley asked.

"It was summer break." Her lip curled as she glanced at Charley before turning back to Mark. "I never forget a face or where I know it from. So, when he turned up here...well, you have to wonder. I thought perhaps he'd been sent for a reason; that I'd been given a mission. But no, he'd just stumbled in where he didn't belong."

"Why do you call him a coward?" Charley

asked. She shifted her gaze to Elliot. "And why don't you dispute it?"

Elliot cracked open an eye and shrugged.

"He deserted his platoon and hid out in Switzerland for the duration of the war," Meredith said. "That's where the Commissariat found him. After they recruited him to the cause, they sent him back to Canada and gave him the identity of a dead kid," Meredith said. "As a deserter, he couldn't have returned to his old life, could he?"

"Now who's got loose lips?" Elliot snarled at Meredith.

"What's your real name?" Freddie stepped closer to the bed and shone his flashlight directly into Elliot's eyes.

"I am not going to tell you." Elliot turned his head away and tried to cross his arms in defiance but only succeeded in pulling Meredith hard against the bed.

"But you're not Elliot Shaw," Charley persisted. "So, why on earth would you agree to come to a place where everyone knows him? Were you sent here to kill Foster Bennett?"

"I didn't kill him." Elliot raised his chin and smirked. "Nobody sent me here. I decided to come on my own as a way to secure my new identity. I had the kid's history. I knew none of you had seen him since he was a kid. You were expecting Elliot Shaw and Elliot Shaw arrived."

"What happens now?" Meredith arched a brow as she regarded Dan. "A tasteful divorce?"

"We keep you here until the police arrive. And then you'll be turned over to the Royal Canadian Mounted Police for interrogation." His expression was impassive and his eyes showed no emotion, but he sounded exhausted.

Mark motioned for Charley, Dan and Freddie to step away from the prisoners. "Freddie and I will take turns guarding them," he said in a low voice.

"I can take a shift," Dan offered.

"Sorry, Sport, but you're too close to this. Let me and the professor handle it." He turned to Freddie. “Can you do the first shift? There’s something I need to discuss with Charley and Dan.”

“Sure thing.” Freddie accepted the revolver Dan handed him and settled himself into an armchair facing the captives. “Hey,” he called out before they left. “Do you think I could light a fire? It’s cold enough to freeze the balls off a brass monkey.”

“Yeah. Looks like there are a few logs here already. That should get you started. I’ll bring more to keep it going when I come for my shift.”

As the three stepped into the hallway, Dan reached out and took Charley’s arm. “I owe you an apology. You were right about Meredith.”

She patted his hand. “It gives me no pleasure.”

Mark put his finger to his lips and ushered them back into room 114. “I have a confession to make,” he said after he closed the door. “I wasn’t completely forthcoming about my reasons for not wanting to use 111 as a listening post.”

"I knew it!" Charley couldn't help herself.

Mark and Dan rolled their eyes in unison. They could fight it all they wanted, but the more time they spent together, the more similarities she saw between them.

"So, let's have it?" Charley said. "Why'd you lie?"

"I didn't lie, exactly. I didn't want to jeopardize Cannon's operation."

"And how would using that room done that?" Dan asked. "We could have gotten vital information if we'd been able to listen in."

"Because room 111 isn't vacant. It seems I'm not the only one living on the first floor."

"There's someone else down here?" Charley asked. The more she thought about it, the more it made sense.

"What makes you think that? Did you see someone?" Dan asked.

"Not exactly," Mark admitted. "When I opened the door to the room, I saw a veritable feast laid out on a table along with a pair of men's boots by the door. I don't know if anyone was there. I didn't go in. I quietly closed the door and came back here to keep watch on the hallway, but I didn't see any movement from that room. Of course, I couldn't cover both the hallway and the patio entrances."

"Well, that's one mystery solved. Now we know what happened to all Bonnie's food," Dan said.

"I thought you took the food," Charley said to Mark. "It disappeared the morning you arrived."

Mark laid his hand across his heart. "You wound me, Tiger. I am much subtler than you give me credit for. If I'd pinched some of your food, you'd never know it."

"Be that as it may," Dan said before Charley could apologize—she should have known better—"who the dickens would it be?"

"It's obvious, isn't it?" Charley asked. She glanced between the two men. Mark nodded in agreement, but Dan's expression was confused. She heaved a sigh. "It's Fraser Bennett. He killed his brother so he could get control over the resort and was then trapped here when the storm moved in."

"Charley—" Dan's eyes narrowed, his skepticism clear.

"It makes sense," Charley insisted. "The will says the brothers must act together. We know Foster wanted to start up the family resort again, but what if Fraser didn't? He spent the last few years looking after his father and taking care of the resort. Maybe he'd had enough. But thanks to that will, he would have been stuck with whatever Foster decided to do with the property. How would he feel? Angry? Angry enough to murder his brother?"

"It's a good theory," Mark said.

"It's speculation," Dan said. "You don't know any of this."

"Then let's go ask him ourselves," Mark said.

"Do you think he's still in there? With all the noise we made right next door?" Charley asked.

Mark shrugged. "Where else is he going to go. No one knows he's here. His safest plan is to lie low until you all leave and then make his escape with no one the wiser."

"I can't believe she's got you convinced Foster was murdered," Dan said.

"Well, if it's not Fraser Bennett, who else could be in that room?" Charley asked.

"Probably no one. Maybe Elliot took the food and was storing it there in case he needed to escape?" Dan turned to Mark. "It would make sense to set up in a separate location from where he was meeting Meredith. That's what I would do."

Mark shrugged. "Maybe. But there's still the office break-in to consider."

"That's the other thing. Why would Fraser have to break into the safe? As an heir, he's entitled to see the will."

Mark withdrew his gun. "There's no need for us to stand around flipping our lips about it when the answer is right across the hall."

Charley picked up the flashlight. "Let's go."

"Whoa, Tiger! No need for all three of us. Cannon can cover the patio entrance and I'll breach the door. You wait here until we've got him subdued."

Charley glared at the two men. "Don't think for one second I am going to let you sideline me. I'm the one who solved this case. Besides," she trained the beam from her flashlight on them, "Dan doesn't have his gun anymore."

"And a flashlight is a good substitute?" Dan asked.

"It'll do in a pinch," she said. She turned to Mark. "You can't keep me out of this."

"All right. But stay behind me."

"You can't be serious about letting her go with us?" Dan said.

"If we don't, then one of us is going to have to stay here and hold her down."

"It's settled." Charley glanced down at her watch. "We'll give you five minutes to get into position."

Dan grabbed his coat from the bed, yanked it over his arms and crammed a wool toque onto his head. "Five minutes," he said as he slipped out the patio door.

"Thank you," Charley said turning to Mark.

Mark held up his hands. "I didn't agree because I wanted to. I'd rather you stay here and let Cannon and me handle this."

"But why? I just helped you take down two spies."

"Sleeper agents aren't true spies," Mark said. "You saw the pair of them; a good stiff wind could blow them over. They're dreamers the commies have taken advantage of. I'm sure they had no proper training before being planted here. If they had, they wouldn't have copped to being 'spies' so quickly. But this Fraser guy? We don't know what we're dealing with. If you're right, he's a killer."

"With poison, not a gun."

"And you think that makes him less dangerous?" Mark raised his eyebrows.

"Less violent, wouldn't you think?"

"Cleverer, though, considering he's managed to convince everyone, except you, that his brother's death was due to natural causes. He's planned this all out; if he thinks it's about to go down the drain, he could become desperate. Unpredictable."

"We've been in dangerous situations before. How is this different?" she asked.

Mark lowered his gaze to his gun to check the cylinder, even though he hadn't fired a single bullet since he'd loaded it earlier in the evening. "I can't be worrying about you and do my job properly at the same time," he said, not looking up.

His concern discomforted her. "You don't need to worry about me. I can handle myself."

When he raised his head, his mouth was

set in a stern, uncompromising line, and his black eyes bore into hers. "If there was another way—*any* other way—you would be staying put."

In the glow of the flashlight's beam, she read fear in his dark eyes. Fear for her. Her heart sank. She thought he had confidence in her, that he respected her—if not quite as an equal, at least enough to see her as a partner. "Well, there is no other way," she said stonily. "And five minutes are about up."

Rather than kicking open the door, Mark quickly picked the lock. They entered quietly, his gun leading the way. Charley waited near the door while he did a quick scan of the room. At his nod, she hurried to open the patio door for Dan while Mark checked out the bathroom. Dan opened the wardrobe and checked under the bed.

No one.

But there was an outdoor coat lying across an armchair, and a pair of men's winter boots sitting beside the food-laden table. He *had* been here.

She picked up the waxed cotton coat and

gasped as all the pieces fell into place. "Recognize this?" she held up the coat for Dan to see.

"A lot of people wear those types of coats," Dan said.

She shook her head. She knew it had to be Fraser who killed Foster, but she still couldn't figure out how he'd pulled it off. Until now. The coat explained everything. "Don't you see, it was Fraser the whole time. Foster was dead before we even arrived."

"How is that possible?" Dan sat down on the edge of the bed and rubbed his eyes. "We all saw him."

Learning of Meredith's deception had taken a lot out of her friend. Charley could tell his confidence had been rocked, and she wished she could do something to help restore it. But he lived in a world of facts and logic, and her trust in intuition was something he'd never understood.

"Why don't you lay out the rest of your theory, Tiger. How do you think things went down?"

Did Mark want her to explain it for Dan's

benefit or did he think there was someone else listening? From the way his eyes were darting around the room and the fact he hadn't holstered his gun, she suspected the latter.

Fraser had grown up here, and if he and his brother were anything like her and Freddie, they'd probably had dozens of hidey-holes throughout the resort. There had to be a reason he'd selected this room to hide in rather than the one next door, furthest away from the reception area.

"Okay." Charley paced over to stand in front of the fireplace, but of course, it hadn't been lit and the cool draft coming down the chimney sent her to the other side of the room. "I think Fraser arrived to confront his brother about the will. One or the other of them wanted to sell the resort—I suspect Fraser—but he couldn't do it without the other's agreement. When Foster refused, Fraser killed him. I don't think he expected the body to be found until later in the spring—remember, the resort never opened this early—but then Bonnie and Carl showed up, and he learned a whole bunch of guests were about to arrive. He was stuck. He had to think fast so he pretended to be Foster."

Charley couldn't stand still anymore and began pacing. "When we arrived, Bonnie said she couldn't find the guest list she'd brought with her. That's because Fraser took it. Remember, we found a list in the bedroom alongside those school yearbooks?"

"Every five years until he got to ours," Dan said.

"Precisely. He was looking for us, so he'd know who was coming. He didn't know I'd been a student at KCI, too, because he'd been looking for my married name, Hall, rather than Stormont."

"That doesn't make any sense," Dan said. "Bonnie and Carl knew both Foster and Fraser. Surely, they'd have realized it was Fraser when they arrived."

"Not necessarily," Charley said. "Carl admitted he hadn't seen the brothers for more than a decade. Remember what Elliot said about expectations? They were expecting Foster, so they'd assume it was Foster who greeted them."

She could see Dan was still struggling to come to her conclusion, so she took a different tack. "What is the one thing all of us remember about Foster Bennett?" Charley asked and then answered. "His beard. We were teenagers, we didn't pay much attention to our teachers, but everyone remembered Mr. Bennett's 'great flowing beard.' Even Bonnie admitted that was how she recognized him when he came to town. If you take that away..."

"But Bonnie said she regularly saw Fraser when he came into the pharmacy for supplies —and had seen him and Foster as recently as a few months ago at their father's funeral. Beard or no beard, surely she'd have realized it was Fraser."

"Possibly, if her eyesight wasn't failing her."

"What? How do you know that?"

"I was trying to figure out why she went into the office looking for a pencil and paper when both were in the reception area.

Then I realized it was because I had moved them away from the telephone, where they usually were, over to the other end of the counter. She couldn't see them. And remember the trouble she had unlocking the office door? I think she couldn't see the keyhole properly. And those headaches she's been having; she needs glasses, but I suspect she can't afford them, which is why the thought of losing this job was so devastating to her."

Dan stood. "So, you think Fraser killed Foster shortly before everyone arrived and then found himself stuck here with us. That would have been Wednesday. But we didn't find Foster's body until Friday. Why wait that long?"

"Alibi. Think about it. Now he has fourteen people who will swear that Foster Bennett was alive and well until at least late Thursday night. So even if anyone knew Fraser had been here on Wednesday, we would all be able to say he'd been long gone before his brother's untimely demise."

"I still don't know, Charley. He'd have to

have been fast on his feet to put it all together so quickly."

"But there were mistakes," Charley said. "Lots of them."

There was a grunt and sanding sound of wood against wood. Charley and Dan whirled to face the source. Mark dropped to his knees and aimed his gun as the wardrobe door swung open.

A false back. She should have thought of that.

"Well done, Mrs. Hall," Fraser Bennett said, slapping his palms together slowly in mocking applause. "But I think your use of the words 'lots' is incorrect."

"Really?" Charley raised an eyebrow.

She couldn't believe she'd managed to draw him out. While she'd had very little interaction with Fraser, it had been enough to know that he considered himself superior to most people, but especially to women. Still, belittling his plan had been a long shot.

"Where do you want me to begin?" she asked, hyping up her disdain. "Perhaps with your most obvious error. Since you passed yourself off as your brother to us, you needed to get rid of Foster's beard. It's not easy to shave another person—and certainly, more challenging when they're already dead. There were no bloody cloths, and there should have been considering how you mangled it. But if Foster was already dead, there'd be no heartbeat to pump out the blood. I might have overlooked all of that but for one crucial error: you forgot to wind the alarm clock."

"Why would that matter?" Fraser asked.

"It wouldn't have on its own. But it seemed odd for someone so meticulous. And that got me thinking about all the other inconsistencies. For example, your sudden, uncontrollable cough right before you retired for the evening. It came out of nowhere and seemed forced. I think you wanted us to think you were ill, so we'd be less suspicious when we found Foster's body the next morning."

"And that's it?" Fraser sneered at her. "A bad shave, a forgotten clock, and a coughing fit?"

"And then there's this." She motioned toward the table with all the food. "Bonnie would have forgiven the odd missing piece of toast or hard-boiled egg—likely wouldn't have even mentioned it—but she couldn't ignore the loss of an entire meal for a dozen people. I kept asking myself, why would any of us bother? We had enough food to last for days. No, whoever took it needed to lay in their own supply because they couldn't count on Bonnie's meals."

Charley kept her gaze focused on Fraser's face. His bloodshot eyes stared back at her through glasses with dark, heavy frames rather than the round wire spectacles that had been his brother's. He hadn't shaved for several days and there were patches of dark grey bristles on his cheeks and chin, making her wonder if he was even capable of growing a beard as full as Foster's had been.

"But it was the office break-in that convinced me that it wasn't one of us who was the murderer. Given the terms of your father's will, you were the most likely suspect. I just wasn't sure how it had all played out until I saw your coat and realized it had been you all along."

Fraser lunged toward her. Before Dan could move to intercept him or Mark could even get off a shot, she whacked him over the head with her flashlight, knocking him back into the wardrobe.

Mark and Dan jumped on him, pulling him to his feet and marching him over to the armchair.

"What did you think you were going to do?" Mark growled. "Take her hostage?"

Fraser rubbed his forehead. An ugly red welt was already forming under the skin. "It was a thought," he muttered.

"Another mistake: underestimating me," Charley said. "I am curious, though. Why did you need to get the will?"

Fraser glanced up at Mark and then Dan, each standing on one side of him. He wasn't going anywhere, and he knew it. "Okay, I'll tell you. Not that it's going to make any difference to you." He made a great pretence of showing off his composure, calmly crossing his legs and leaning back in his chair, as if settling in for a good story. "My 'perfect' brother was never around. I was the one who came here every summer to help run the resort. And when our parents got sick, I was the one who took care of them—first helping my mother and then assuming full responsibility for my father after she'd passed."

"Did you know what was in the will before they died?" Charley asked.

"No, but for some reason Foster did." He leaned forward. "Let me make this clear: I was happy to care for our parents. I didn't expect anything special for it."

"But you also didn't expect to be tied to whatever decision Foster made about this place," Charley said.

"I couldn't believe it when he told me he wanted to reopen Bennett's Family Resort—turn it into some sort of summer sports camp for boys. I said, 'fine, buy me out.' I was done with this place."

"Then he told you about the will."

"Yeah. He said I was stuck, that he couldn't buy me out even he wanted to, which he didn't anyway, the cheap so-and-so."

"You couldn't walk away? Leave it all to him?" Charley asked.

Fraser shook his head. "I'm broke. Everything I'd saved was spent taking care of our parents. I quit my job, sold my house. I was counting on the money we'd get from selling this place. Foster had never shown any interest in it. Heck, for years he never even came here—and he should have since he had his summers off."

"So, you came up here to kill him?"

"No. Yes? Maybe?" Fraser shrugged. "I don't know. I thought he was lying and the will didn't say what he said it did. He'd been named executor, not me. I didn't trust him and when I asked to see the will, he showed me the safe he'd purchased and said it was safe-and-sound in there and if I wanted to contest it, I should get a lawyer—as if I could afford that."

"He wasn't lying about the will," Charley said.

"It doesn't matter anymore. With him gone, it's all mine now."

"Not if you're convicted of his murder," Dan said.

Fraser crossed his arms, smugly confident.

"I won't be convicted. No one is going to believe your crazy story. So, what if you found me hiding here? I'll tell them I didn't feel like socializing with a bunch of my brother's former students. All you have is speculation. There's not a shred of evidence to *prove* Foster died by my hand."

"Have you told him yet?" Freddie asked. He reached out and took the towel-wrapped ice pack from Charley's hand and pressed it against the back of his head.

"Yes, he knows. I don't think I've ever seen Dan so angry before," Charley said.

"I'm really sorry. I let you all down."

"Don't be silly. It's me who should be apologizing to you. We shouldn't have left you to guard them by yourself." Charley stopped herself from wrapping her arms around her brother again. She'd been so frightened when they found him unconscious.

Freddie cocked his head to the side and then winced in pain. "I had a gun. And they weren't going anywhere—or so we thought."

After they'd captured Fraser, they decided to put him with Meredith and Elliot while they waited for the police to arrive. Charley had gone to get Carl to help guard the three suspects, while Mark and Dan moved Fraser to the next room.

When they arrived in room 113, they found Freddie lying unconscious by the fireplace and Elliot the only other occupant.

Now that he'd been abandoned by his co-conspirator, Elliot was much more talkative. He told them Colin had snuck up on Freddie while he'd been building a fire and hit him over the head with the butt of a gun he'd brought with him. Then he'd managed to unlock Meredith's handcuff and secured the empty bracelet around the metal arched headboard.

Elliot had begged to be released, too, but he had the sense that Colin wasn't rescuing Meredith out of duty to their cause. From the conversation he'd overheard, Colin wasn't a Soviet sympathizer; his only concern was for his sister. He hadn't even taken Dan's revolver with them. He'd left it on the floor beside Freddie.

"Here you go, dear," Bonnie handed

Freddie a cup of tea. "Are you sure I can't put a little brandy in? It might help."

Charley held her breath, but Freddie easily refused Bonnie's offer.

The rest of the guests were slowly making their way into the dining room, roused by the arrival of a large snowplough, followed by two police squad cars. Apparently, Chuck had been very persuasive and the ploughing of the road to the resort had begun late last evening.

Dan and Mark had accompanied Elliot and Fraser back to Port Perry in those squad cars. Now, they were waiting for a medical examiner to arrive before moving Foster's body. Several other officers had remained behind and were taking statements from everyone. They were currently interviewing Trixie in the lounge.

Hal sat down across the table from Charley, but he wouldn't meet her eyes. "I guess I owe you an apology."

"That's not necessary," she said.

"Still, you were right about Foster being

murdered." He looked up. "Maybe when we get back to Kingston we can try—"

Charley placed her hand on his to stop him from continuing. "It won't work, and we both know it."

He gazed down at her hand over his and sighed. Failure wasn't something Hal was used to. "But we can still be friends, can't we?"

"Of course." She squeezed his hand. "No hard feelings." She was willing to be magnanimous, especially now that she'd been proven right.

"Spies! Did I hear there were Communist secret agents among us?" Pamela called out gleefully as she pulled over a chair from the adjacent table. "Imagine! I was friends with one. You must tell us every little detail, Charley! Are you going to write about this? Will I be in the *Tribune*?"

Freddie's eyebrows rose and his hand holding his teacup stalled partway to his lips.

Charley gave him a reassuring smile and turned to face the group that had assembled around them. "No. I won't be writing anything about this for the *Tribune*. It's not a story for the women's pages. But I will tell you what happened yesterday and early this morning."

"That's quite a story," Ralph said when she'd finished. "But it's all circumstantial, isn't it? If there was no obvious sign of foul play on the body, how will the police prove Fraser killed his brother?"

"Hopefully, an autopsy will help with that," Charley said.

"How did he kill Foster?" Pamela asked.

"I think Fraser somehow subdued his brother and then injected him with an overdose of insulin. I found a tiny red mark under his arm."

"Insulin? Oh yes, he'd have had easy access to that," Bonnie said from the back of the group. "His father was a diabetic."

"Precisely," Charley said. "I realized that when you told me about his ailments. And as his father's caregiver, Fraser would have known the consequences of giving too much."

"There is one thing I still don't understand," Carl said. "When we found Foster, the door was locked from the inside. I had to break down the bloody thing—forgive my language, ladies."

"Figuring out the locked room was the easiest part of all this." Charley's eyes roamed the room as her audience leaned in closer. She was enjoying drawing out their suspense probably more than she should. But after enduring their derision for the last few days it felt good to have been proven correct.

"You never said anything," Hal countered.

"What was the point? You wouldn't believe me when I showed you the obvious signs that Foster was murdered; I didn't think explaining how the killer got out would change your mind."

She turned to Freddie and pointed to the wet towel he'd placed on the table. He slid it across to her and she unwrapped it, withdrawing a melting cube. "Ice. Or, I suppose it could have been packed snow. Whichever it was, Fraser wedged it under the door handle. As it melted, the handle came down and sealed the room."

Charley looked up at Carl. "I don't think Fraser anticipated how cold the room was going to get. He likely assumed there'd only be a small damp spot on the floor in the morning, which no one would notice. But because the power had gone off, the melted liquid re-froze and created that slippery patch that we all had to be careful of."

"Oh, bravo, Charley," Pamela said. "You've solved it all."

"Yes, here's to Charley!" Sam Winn stood and began clapping. He was quickly joined by the rest of the guests as well as Bonnie and Carl. A chorus of "well dones" accompanied the applause.

Charley's cheeks warmed at the ovation. "There is still one thing I haven't been able to figure out," she admitted when the accolades finished. "Why did Foster invite you all here to begin with?"

"Oh!" Freddie flushed. "I think I can answer that. Give me a minute."

He stood unsteadily and Charley leapt to her feet and rounded the table, taking his arm to help him.

"I'll be fine." He pried her fingers off his

forearm and made his way out of the dining room on unsteady feet.

Charley turned to Hal in alarm.

"I'll go with him to see if he needs a hand," he said and followed Freddie.

It felt like an eternity before the two men returned. Hal was carrying Freddie's suitcase. He placed it on the table and stepped back while Freddie unclipped the two metal locks and lifted the lid. Light glinted off a long, smooth object—the one Charley had feared was a bottle of whiskey when she'd seen it back in his bedroom in Kingston. As he picked it up, she realized it was a metal scabbard with the wooden handle of some sort of dagger extending out of it.

"Is that...?" Hal began.

"I don't believe it!" Ralph leaned in to take a closer look.

Freddie withdrew a six-inch dagger and laid it on the table beside the scabbard. An Imperial German Eagle was engraved on the blade up near the handle.

"Theo and I spent most of that spring camp

hunting for it. I always suspected Benny knew we were the ones who'd nicked it, but he never said anything. Frankly, I'd pretty much forgotten about it until I found it among Theo's things after I came home from the war. I brought it here, intending to give it back to Benny. It wasn't until Cannon pointed out who all was here that I realized that getting back his dagger was probably the point of the invitation."

Sam picked up the dagger and turned it over in his hand. "It sure is a beauty. I betcha it's worth a pretty penny now."

"It's back where it belongs finally." Freddie took it from Sam and turned it over in his hands. "Benny took great pride in this dagger. It reminded him of a very important time in his life. You could tell that from the way he held it, the stories he told about it, how he tried to use it to instill a sense of personal pride in us—however misguided. I shall always be sorry I wasn't able to give it back to him." He looked up at Carl. "I think he'd like to be buried with it. Can you see to that?"

"Yes, sir." Carl carefully took the dagger and slid it back into the scabbard.

Trixie returned, her face flushed. "Did I miss anything?" she asked when she saw everyone gathered around a single table.

"Nah." Sam wrapped his arm around her. "I'll fill you in on the way home." He turned toward the police officer who'd followed Trixie into the dining room. "We can go now, can't we?"

"As soon as I've taken your statement, you are free to leave," the constable replied.

"C'mon, baby. Let's get out of here." Sam took Trixie's arm and led her from the room.

"Can I go next?" Bob asked and trailed the officer out of the room. The others quickly dispersed, anxious to be on their way. Bonnie and Carl disappeared through the swinging door to the kitchen.

"I guess we can go, too," Hal said to Charley and Freddie. "We've all spoken with the authorities. I'll run up and get our bags."

"I am going to wait for Mark and Dan to get back," Charley said. "I'll catch a ride with one of them."

Hal frowned. “Are you sure? You don’t know how long they’ll be.”

She gave him a reassuring smile. “I’m sure. Thank you.”

“I know you said things are okay between us, but…well, it’s a small world and—”

“We’ll always be friends, Hal. I wouldn’t have it any other way.”

He took a step back and glanced down at his boots before meeting her gaze once more. “Okay,” he said, hesitantly. “I guess I’ll be seeing you around.”

“I’ll be with you in a jiffy,” Freddie said.

Hal nodded and strode from the room.

Freddie placed a gentle kiss on Charley’s cheek. “You did a great job here. I wish we’d all been a little more supportive.”

“Next time you’ll know better. You better get going. You don’t want to keep Hal waiting.”

“I’m not sure my job here is done. As your chaperone, maybe I should stick around for when the two gentlemen return.” He wiggled his eyebrows suggestively.

“Don’t be silly.” Charley swatted his arm

playfully. “It’s a simple car ride back to Kingston.”

“Yes, but who will be the lucky chauffeur? Will it be the dashing young politician with a wounded heart? Or the dark, brooding detective who is only now discovering he has a heart?”

Indeed. That was the question, wasn’t it?

"Can I get you a bowl of soup?"

Charley looked up from *Tottel's Miscellany*. The *Songes and Sonnets* of Thomas Wyatt, Henry Howard, and their compatriots were more interesting than she'd expected them to be—at least they were helping her pass the time while she waited for Mark and Dan to return from Port Perry. "Yes, please, Bonnie. Will you join me?"

Bonnie returned from the kitchen carrying a tray with two steaming bowls of potato soup and thick fresh-from-the-oven slices of bread.

"The hydro men have arrived," Bonnie said. "They told Carl it would likely take a week to repair all the damaged lines and restore power."

"Will you stay on here?"

"I think so; for now, at least. I don't like

the idea of leaving the place empty, especially once the story of what happened here gets out." She blew on the spoonful of soup she'd scooped up. "You know how nosy people can be."

"Yes. I don't imagine you get many murders and Soviet spies, never mind both in the same place at the same time." Charley tore off a chunk of her bread and dipped it into her bowl. "What about the longer term? Will you and Carl be all right?"

"Oh, certainly. I can go back to working at the pharmacy and there are always people needing a big, strong man like Carl. It's just..."

Charley reached across the table and took her hand. "Maybe whoever buys the place will want to keep it as a family resort, so you won't have to be separated as often."

"Perhaps."

But Charley knew it wasn't only the prospect of losing this job that had Bonnie most concerned. "Have you seen a doctor about your eyesight?"

Bonnie stared into her bowl.

"I'd like to help if you'll let me."

Bonnie's head shot up and her eyes rounded, appalled. The chair scraped along the floor as she pushed it back and stood. "Oh, no, Mrs. Hall. Carl and I don't need any charity."

"It's not charity," Charley said, standing, too. "My family… I have so much it seems wrong not to share it where it could be of help."

It was as if Bonnie's face turned to stone—mottled crimson and white, like the coarse-grained granite of the Canadian Shield. Her hands shook as she collected their bowls, and Charley watched in dismay as she carried them, rattling on the tray, back into the kitchen.

Charley sighed, picked up the book and wandered through to the lounge. There were a few embers still glowing in the fireplace, but with everyone gone, there wasn't the urgency to keep it well-stoked. She replaced the book where it should have always been—English literature, subsection poetry—tossed a log onto the fire, and curled herself into one of the armchairs.

She'd done it again, but what "it" was, she couldn't figure out. What was so wrong with offering to help Bonnie? The Stormont family supported all sorts of organizations that assisted those in need. How was this any different?

She could ask Mark. He was good at pointing out her failings when it came to dealing with people from different backgrounds. But her offer to Bonnie had been made with the best of intentions and she cringed at the thought of him mocking her for it.

Charley was too exhausted to try to figure it all out now. She closed her eyes for just a moment and the next thing she knew the room had darkened, the fire had died and someone had placed a blanket over her. She sat up, wincing at the twinge in her back. She'd gotten no sleep last night, so it was no wonder she'd dozed off. But she was surprised to see the clock on the mantel telling her it was close to six o'clock, dinner time. Her stomach rumbled, confirming the late hour.

She stood, stretched and headed to the kitchen. She still didn't know why her offer had offended Bonnie, but at the very least, she should offer her an apology.

Charley recognized two of the deep masculine voices coming from the dining room.

"There she is," Dan said at the same time as Mark called out, "Well, hello, Sleeping Beauty."

Across the table from them were two uniformed police officers.

"I'll be right back," she said and passed through to the kitchen.

Bonnie looked up when she entered. She pulled her arms out of a basin of soapy water and dried them on a towel. "Did you sleep, all right?" she asked. "I meant to come back and add another log to the fire for you but—"

"I slept very well. Thank you for the blanket," Charley said. "About earlier..."

"No need to discuss it," Bonnie said quickly. "Now, all I have to offer you for dinner is more soup, I'm afraid."

"That sounds lovely. I'll help myself."

Charley carried a bowl to the stove and ladled it full of Bonnie's delicious potato soup.

Charley took her bowl to the table and sat down across from Mark and Dan. Neither of them had slept last night, either, but they didn't look nearly as exhausted as she still felt. Dan introduced her to the constables—Arculus and Dougall. There were more, he said, combing through the bedrooms that had been occupied by Foster, Elliot and Colin, as well as his own, of course.

"What happened in Port Perry?" she asked.

"There will be an autopsy on Foster, but if it is an insulin overdose as you suspect, that may be hard to prove, and Fraser isn't saying anything," Mark said.

"We'll keep on him," Arculus, the older of the pair, said. "I'm sure we can get him to break soon enough."

"And Elliot?" She turned to Dan.

"The RCMP have him now. It won't be long before they find out his real name. And they've launched a fugitive hunt for Meredith and Colin." Dan's voice was monotone, and he wouldn't look at her directly.

"They won't get far," Dougall said with an arrogance that reminded Charley of another young constable. "We've frozen all their bank accounts."

"The ones you know about, anyway," Mark said. "I wouldn't be surprised if Meredith had some money stashed away somewhere. She's a pretty sharp cookie."

"Fooled me," Dan said.

"Don't be so hard on yourself. You were looking in the wrong place," Charley said. "It made more sense for Colin to be the spy. You had no reason to suspect Meredith."

"Yet you did," Dan said.

"I didn't suspect her. I couldn't warm up to her, that's all," Charley said.

"Don't sell yourself short, Tiger. You've got great intuition, as you so ably demonstrated with both the Bennett murder and ID'ing Elliot and Meredith as sleeper agents."

"I wonder if that wasn't more a matter of dumb luck," Charley said.

"What are you talking about?" Mark said.

It had been gnawing at her ever since Meredith had mentioned the coincidence of her and "Elliot" being in the same place at the same time. "We always say there's no such thing as coincidence, but everything that happened was built on coincidence. The only reason we found Fraser was because we were tracking Elliot. And the only reason I was tracking Elliot was that I suspected he was involved in Foster's murder. But the two cases had nothing to do with each other."

"You're over-thinking this," Mark said. "You suspected Foster was murdered, and you were right. You suspected there was something fishy about this Elliot Shaw character, and you were right about that, too. Okay, so the cases aren't related, but you see things that others miss. I'd bet a million bucks that you would have solved both cases, even if they hadn't been blurred together. Face it, Tiger, some things are simply meant to be."

She gave Mark an appreciative smile. Maybe he was right but if that was the case, it must mean some things weren't meant to be, too.

Dan pushed his chair back. "It's getting late. I think we should be heading back to Kingston." He looked at Charley. "Do you need help with your bag?"

"No, I brought it down earlier. It's behind the reception counter. I'll go get it."

Charley slipped on her winter coat and carried her blue tartan suitcase out to the parking lot.

Mark was leaning casually against his black sedan. "You travel light," he said straightening. He held out his hand to take her bag, but she held onto it. He cocked his head and frowned. "What's up?"

"I can't tell you how grateful I am that you came for me and believed in me when no one else did, but I'm not going to drive back with you," she said. "I'll catch up with you in Kingston." She turned and walked away before she could read his expression. Would he be hurt? Angry? She didn't want to know.

It was only a car ride, but it threatened to become so much more. Even if Grace was right and Mark did have feelings for her, even if he wasn't a man who would insist his wife stay home, was this a relationship she wanted? Yes, he believed in her and encouraged her to see the world differently, but he wasn't always sympathetic when she stumbled.

She couldn't help that she'd been born to wealth and privilege. So yes, she made mistakes. And yes, she didn't understand why an offer to help someone less fortunate was so offensive. But why couldn't Mark accept that she was trying her best? Why must he make her feel as though she were guilty of something she had no control over? Trying to live up to his expectations was exhausting.

She could feel his black eyes boring into her back as she walked across the parking lot toward Dan and his Woody.

She almost cried at the relief she saw on her best friend's face. Dear, sweet Dan. His self-confidence was shaken, but not shattered—at least she hoped not. It was clear he was dreading the long, lonely trip home, but that was exactly what he needed: time on his own so he could come to terms with what had happened and begin to think about his future.

"I won't drive home with you, Dan," Charley said as she approached. "I will help you get through this, I promise. But right now, it's best if we each take some time, alone, to sort ourselves out." She stood on her tiptoes and kissed his cheek. "You will always be my dearest friend." She just didn't know if he could ever be anything more.

She continued past him, stopping beside the idling police cruiser. She rapped on the window. "Can you take me to the bus station in Port Perry? Bonnie said there's a coach leaving at eight that will get me to Kingston."

Charley slid into the back seat, leaned back and closed her eyes, feeling at peace with herself for the first time in a very long while. She didn't know what the future held, but she did know, with absolute certainty, that she would be the one to write it.

Want to know more about Charley and the gang?

Head over to my website to subscribe to *The Gayle Gazette* for details about future releases, contests & giveaways, and all manner of shenanigans including a free download of the mini-mystery *To Fetch a Thief* (A Bessie Stormont Whodunit) and members-only access to *Charley's Field Notes*, a peek into the inspirations for Charley's world.
www.BrendaGayle.com

Thank you for taking this journey with me. I hope these books have given you as much joy reading them as they have me writing them.

Historical Notes

Schooled in Murder is a work of fiction, but as with all of the Charley Hall Mystery books, I like to include as much historically accurate information as possible. For example, there was a total eclipse of the full moon on April 13, 1949, which was visible throughout Canada. And while my previous books have provided accurate depictions of the weather at the time of the stories, I'm afraid I deviated from that for this adventure. Although the days just prior to Easter were unseasonably warm, there was not a major ice storm around Lake Scugog that weekend. But, as a survivor of the Great Ice Storm of 1998, I do have vivid memories of what such events are like. The descriptions of the aftermath, including the sound of ice-laden branches shattering as they fall to the ground, are true to life.

Camp X

Camp X was the unofficial name of the paramilitary training installation established on the shore of Lake Ontario, between Whitby and Oshawa, thirty miles straight across from the United States border. Its purpose was to provide a strategic link between Britain and the United States, which, until the attack on Pearl Harbor, was forbidden by Congress to get involved in the war. Ironically, Camp X opened on December 6, 1941—the day before the infamous attack.

The camp was set up by British Security Co-ordination Chief Sir William Stephenson, a Canadian from Winnipeg, Manitoba. Stephenson is best known by his wartime intelligence codename Intrepid, and many consider him to be one of the real-life inspirations for Ian Fleming's James Bond.

The site of Camp X is now called Intrepid Park. It's marked by a historic plaque dedicated to its history as well as an adjacent one for spymaster William Stephenson.

If you're interested in learning more, I highly recommend Lynn Philip Hodgson's *Inside Camp X*, which tells the story of the genesis of North America's first secret spy school as well as many engrossing tales about the "students" who trained there.

For a fun read, you might also want to pick up *Camp X*, a young adult novel by Eric Walters, which features two young brothers who discover the camp in 1942 and then get swept up in all sorts of intrigue.

Soviet Spies in Canada & the Cold War

Igor Sergeyevich Gouzenko (January 26, 1919 – June 25, 1982) was a cipher clerk for the Soviet Union's embassy in Canada.
He defected on September 5, 1945, three days after the end of World War II, with 109 documents detailing Russia's espionage activities in the West.

Gouzenko exposed Soviet intelligence's

efforts to steal nuclear secrets as well as the technique of planting sleeper agents. The "Gouzenko Affair" is often credited as the trigger for the Cold War.

Camp X was used by the Royal Canadian Mounted Police as a secure location for interviewing Gouzenko. He and his family spent two years at the facility.

Acknowledgements

I can't believe this is book 6 in the Charley Hall historical mystery series. Writing these stories has been such a joy. I couldn't have done it without the full support my wonderful husband, Bruce Legg. An avid reader and someone who usually figures out the whodunit pretty quickly, I let him read early drafts of these books and am gratified (and surprised) when I manage to stump him.

Thanks, as always, to the two talented women who polish my drafts to make them fit for publication. Joanna D'Angelo, my friend and editor, who suggested I write a mystery series and brainstormed ideas with me during a long drive to Toronto and back—and then hounded me until I actually wrote it. And Carolyn Heald, a historian, archivist and gifted writer in her own right, she is also—and truly fortunate for me—an excellent copy editor who is very familiar with the city of Kingston as well as proper grammar.

I am grateful for the support from the great team at Best Page Forward and my fellow students at Author Ad School, who have taught me so much about the self-publishing world.

I'd also like to give a shout-out to the readers of my newsletter, *The Gayle Gazette*, who I can always count on to help me out when I'm in a bind. This book is no exception. Titles aren't my *forte*, so when I was struggling to come up with one, I put out a call to the Gayle Gazetters for suggestions. And boy did they rise to the challenge! In the end, I could only choose one and so a huge thank you to Alice Hazelbaker, who came up with *Schooled in Murder*.

Finally, I want to express my sincere appreciation to the members of the Women's Fiction Writers Association, Crime Writers of Canada and Ottawa Romance Writers, who provide unconditional support and a safe space to ask questions in this strange world of fiction writing.

About Brenda Gayle

I've been a writer all my life but returned to my love of fiction after more than 20 years in the world of corporate communications—although some might argue there is plenty of opportunity for fiction-writing there, too. I have a Master's degree in journalism and an undergraduate degree in psychology. A fan of many genres, I find it hard to stay within the publishing industry's prescribed boxes. Whether it's historical mystery, romantic suspense, or women's fiction, my greatest joy is telling memorable stories with compelling characters.

Connect with me on my website BrendaGayle.com & sign up for *The Gayle Gazette,* my newsletter, to keep up-to-date on new releases, giveaways, and all sorts of shenanigans. And don't forget, as a subscriber, you'll get exclusive access to *Charley's Field Notes* and all of the *Bessie Stormont Whodunits*.

Until next time...

www.BrendaGayle.com

Also by Brenda Gayle

Charley Hall Mystery series

A Shot of Murder

Rigged for Murder

A Diagnosis of Murder

Odds on Murder

Murder in Abstract

Schooled in Murder

Made in United States
Orlando, FL
19 December 2023